THE LONELINESS NETWORK

The Loneliness Network
Book I: Agnostic

Eduardo B. Machado
MMXVII

For the one who someday will bring on some light to a haunted heart.

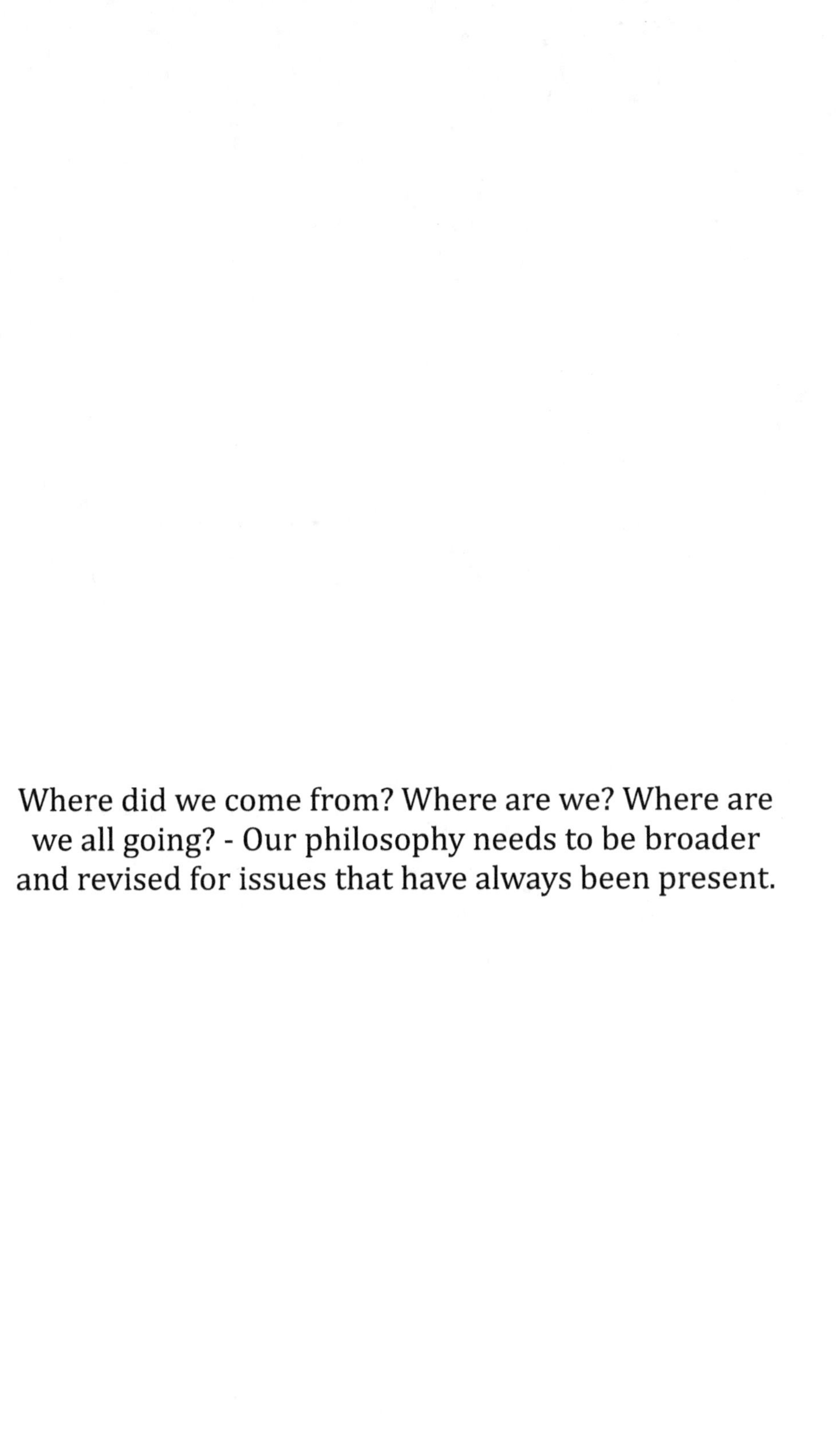

Where did we come from? Where are we? Where are
we all going? - Our philosophy needs to be broader
and revised for issues that have always been present.

Preface

Get ready to read about loneliness. About how much human beings can become fragile and accessible, lost in this sensation. Prepare to look on lines of a really fantastic story, some situated between the real world, the one we see, and the virtual world, the one we do imagine.

Every day millions of people are trying to insert into the virtual world their impressions and concrete facts they have lived through. Social networks are filled with life, hopes and the imagination of beings who have tried to connect these two worlds.

Where would people's lives be, within their imagination, or within a network of interconnected computers? In this lack of what is more alive and vibrant, the reality would no longer depend on a body that walks and breathes.

Don't get it wrong! The virtual world is trying, in the same way, to make the real world fill with its ideas and experiences. In a two way portal, they take an advantage over ordinary users. They are connected in a frame while we are connected in a network.

1st Week

She didn't realize the afternoon had gone already, until a shadow covered the bench where she sat. It was past five o'clock PM, and she could see no more than a red glare of sun behind the sad buildings with dark and empty windows around that square.

She looked at the watch and confirmed: she was late! She might be in the classroom in exactly fifteen minutes. But where has her sense of time gone? It was a mental question she was articulating as she gathered her papers against the wind.

"Yes, I was so punctual one day!" - She thought quietly, in a mixture of reprisal and irony about that situation. If her mouth smiled yellow, her eyes became gray and distant. It was only Tuesday, and for the second time she would be late for histology and cytology classes. Not that they were bad, or the teacher was bored... She just couldn't focus on her studies at all.

She was only nineteen years old and left her small city to study "medicine" in the capital, by her relatives only guess. In fact, she got only credits to apply to nursing college. Even though she was very studious, maybe something got wrong and she lost some chances. She never let herself be impressed by her natural beauty, both envied for all and barely exploited by her. Her name is Patricia, and as her father's pride, she carried only her name, Chase.

During that first month of college, she had imagined herself wearing a white coat with her name embroidered by the pocket. And sometimes she "hears" her name being called in the university's dorm-speaker circuit. Dreams that were becoming more and more insipid, near the dull classes of the first semester. Or would it be because of her choices? Unlike her classmates, who were increasingly lively and anxious, her enthusiasm had run out from the first classes. That was the dream of her maternal grandmother and her father's, not hers!

Since the death of her mother, three months after giving birth, as her only child, father and Gramma Sarah have worked together to care for her, from childhood to the present day. For them there was no difference between that crying little girl, who looked like she was *not-going-to-eat-anything*, to the current woman, who called attention to the slender lines and short hair.

Her father had always given the necessary attention and financial care, as well, but it was her grandmother who performed all the caresses and pampering the girl needed. She called her daughter, as always, and saw in it the real expression of her deceased daughter, although this young version was sadder and farther away than her mother.

For sure, all of her father's effort to surround her with incentives was related to the loss of his wife. His daughter was a chance to remember Laura, no matter how much it hurt, or it takes to make her become a doctor. If there was a doctor in the family, people would probably be cured and not die early. He never said it clearly, but in her daughter's decision to pursue a career, imposed her opinion on medicine. Issues of security, professional achievement, and success were replaced with requests that she would be a good doctor and heal sick people, especially those she loved to.

By age eleven she had already adhered to her father's dreams of doing "medicine" and becoming a doctor, but her decision would not be early enough to see the grandmother's death three years later from a fulminating stroke. Her graduation would not bring these people back, but she could still reciprocate the care and attention of the retired father and sooner or later he should take greater care.

Already in the corridor that leads to the classroom, she had the impression of seeing the silhouette of her grandmother! A countenance of Gramma Sarah at first, but that in the blink of an eye disappeared, revealing the same look she encountered when she found her grandmother dead that afternoon of her death. Her crooked twisted eyes, the twisted mouth, her skin yellowish and cold. She shivered! But she tried to pretend that it was a kind of protection. Somehow energetic, "Candy" as she used to call would be near her.

As she opened the door, she felt a flurry of glances in her direction with the most diverse interests and reprimands. They were in a darkened room with slides of human flesh showing different tissues and since nothing was being spoken, there was the sensation of a sudden interruption in that world. The professor's gaze was initially punitive, but when he saw who was, he changed the countenance to something half-inviting and encouraging.

She sat up hurriedly and opened the laptop. As she hung up the cellphone, she noticed that it had been twenty-three minutes after class began. *"Oh my God, how could I have been late like this..."* She was mortified at criticism. Her day had finally ended, nothing could bring her any more interest or pleasure. She thought of betraying the dreams of everyone, her father, her grandmother, and even her mother who knew only by photos, she guessed. She was to blame for the delays, her performance, her mistakes, and if she failed, she would probably lock up and give up on the course that was killing her.

It was not the course itself. The less she knew, but it was a set of factors. Her wrong choices, life in another city, in another rhythm, living in a boarding house of students, where each one brought different customs and habits, even accents and grimaces that were strange and reprehensible, but the fact that they were studying in an institution. In fact, only parties and drunks would be able to tune in and align such personal differences.

She was sitting next to her mates of the boarding house, but only after a few moments of internal lamentation, she looked around and to receive the smiles of Rudolph and the look of concern of Milena.

Rudolph seemed to be from a neighboring town. Already set in that institution, with the big city and the situation of living away from his family. *"The more freedom the better,"* he commented one day. He was studious and very clever. He also had a strong moral behavior, but his emotional performance, somehow shy for his age. He, as an older man, was a kind of counselor for both. But Milena knew him much longer than Patricia.

Milena was just like Patricia, but a little bit older. Single daughter and coming from another city from the north. She had a hard childhood and even with the incentives of the government, she didn't need scholarships or social programs to get through with the results. She noticed it once. With semi-literate parents, she can overcome prejudices and barriers to be there and share with Patricia her anguish and apprehensions as much as her immediate present of terms and systems as to a professional future. The amount of worry and concern they pay for a college degree. It was so clear they desired everything to be alright, even if it was four years from now. She's doing quite well, even though in some other plan.

Just close to the moment of the end of class, she could hear the voice of Milena breaking her silent concentration. As if invited by a sweet and gentle voice, back to a reality so present and at the same time so distant. She responded only with a shrug when asked why she was late that night.

She didn't know for sure. She was so focused on her readings and memories that she can't tell which one made her to be late on that Tuesday too. Living and being able only to study, delays become less justifiable. Due to her situation, she must be in the classroom at the very first moment when classes begin.

It was twenty minutes to nine o'clock PM and it was time for the class to be declared ended by the teacher. There was a deafening roar of voices and laughter as they all stored their belongings. So a being called Rudolph approached and greeted Patricia with something very much like a kiss on the cheek.

- Hey Paty, my darling?! I thought you won't come today, did you?

- Barely! – (Laughs) She was very nice to him, enough to force him to be social.

- Ready for the second class? Or can we get a snack first on the way? - He was able to talk to her, while Milena gently approached them.

- That's! Food. Let's nourish our cells and increase our fat tissue! She smiled, causing everyone to laugh too.

The two of them went arm in arm with Rudolph to the center. They went out in search of food, inspiration and will to overcome their future so distant and at the same time so present. Anyone who saw Patricia's calm, serene countenance could see that she was quiet and confident, walking through those corridors. Living a life to face and beat death itself.

2nd Week

After her first recorded absence, during the first month of studies, which occurred the previous Wednesday, she stayed in her bed thinking about how futile and petty she had been with her friend Milena.

Milena in the previous morning tried to wake her up in her usual study time, as usually happens daily during this period of adaptation to the course. Milena has always been a disciplined and hard-working being. She was proud of the performance before her superiors. But Patricia, because of her anxiety, could no longer sleep well that night. Result: she woke up more and more unwell for this hour of study with Milena, and for the last three days, she needed to be wrenched out of bed.

"*She only wishes the best for me.*" - She concluded, and so she thought the words she had directed to the newly acquired well-meaning friend were very selfish. They echoed inside her head:

- "You're just waking me up to be your company!" - She spoke in a very serious tone, more than usual. That was a cold and quick voice to her friend who was standing in the doorway of her room, not quite understanding that scene. It sounded like someone else talking, not her friend Patricia.

And also completed aloud:

- "What do you want? Show me I can be a good student?" - It sounded like an outburst, but she tried to defend herself in some way to Milena's insistent behavior.

Patricia, after uttering those words, turned to her pillow, feeling it to try to go back to sleep. Her consciousness was satisfied by the declaration of limits for Milena. *Who does she think she is anyway?"*

Granted that besides Milena being disappointed with Patricia and hurt at the tone of her friend's speech, Patricia had concluded that it was so tough and somehow she should apologize to her friend. Pain and remorse occupied her thoughts in favor of a situation of reconciliation between them. She kept reminiscing and was tormented by the harsh speech of the previous morning. And because she didn't have the physical conditions to go to class last night, she lay down until nine o'clock AM thinking about the fact.

A shade of the relationship between the two of them was shaken a little, was that Milena arrived at the door of Patricia's room at the usual time of study, touched the knob and had a bad impression and did not try to open and wake the friend from sleep. She could suffer even greater threats and sour the relationship between them.

"Better not..." she thought. Patricia had a headache, so she wouldn´t go to class yesterday. Letting her sleep until later seemed like a wise decision.

Inside, there was a still darkened room, Patricia was lying in a fetal position, trying to recover a few more minutes of sleep from a restless night's sleep. It seemed to feel very cold, even with two winter blankets over her.

As she was not woken up by Milena, she had time to try to remember her dreams and how she should apologize to her friend. It all seemed confused and mixed up. She was having difficulty concentrating and focusing on the urgency of the facts. The lost hours of sleep were charging a small price to Patricia. To the point of blending her emotions, nearly into the recent past, hindering the vision of her goals for that day. It seemed that she had not slept that night and everything was still alive in her brain.

She decided to get up, go to college, try to have lunch there and study at the library. Some contents were presented in the previous class. If she saw Milena there, as if that were not possible, she would apologize to her. *"Yes that's it I wanna do!"* She threw the sheets aside and went straight to the bathroom to start up her day. It seemed that she had assimilated the situation and got over it.

Arriving at college, about eleven o'clock AM, she went straight to the cafeteria in an attempt to solve her breakfast problem. She picked up her usual snack and went to find a place to sit in the middle of all the busy tables. She looked quickly at each vacant place, but noticing who would be by her side, sharing that moment… She preferred to give up and to continue walking with her tray. As if she already knew the direction and the place where wanted to sit.

She saw faces and people. Saw their clothes and laughed. People spoke so loudly and gesticulated when they ate. I saw obese students with their mouths full of food. Fancy gorgeous with their perfect hair. Men with smiles of intention as they offered places to sit. With each step, Patricia seemed more disappointed with everyone and astonished in front of that parade of human imperfections. Vanity, envy, gluttony... That was all out there. Everything being presented and paraded in her mind imagined and felt ills that made that sunny morning something somewhat gray and cold. She could no longer focus on anything besides the loud sound of people talking about their deeds and futile laughter that were choked with strident laughter. "*Yes! They think they are happy, but they are desperate to continue living.*" She thought heard her own voice saying that.

She saw the intended place, the only table completely empty. Furthest from all, the dirtiest place on that feeding patio. From where she could see everyone else, but would not be noticed by anyone. She wanted peace and quiet to complete her snack without sharing space, or commenting with strangers about her performance.

She finally sat down with satisfaction to be free of them all. But it seemed that a long way had taken away the warmth and flavor of her snack. She bit off just once to feel the hunger is over. It tasted sour. She took her juice and put more sugar in it. As she drank that sweeter result, she heard a familiar voice right behind her. It was Rudolph who carried some things that seemed like books under his arm. Her first reaction was beckon the call without turning around, she would ask him to leave. But she controlled the words and looked slowly at him. Yes, it was Rudolph himself, she knew his clothes and his manners and knew he was ready to study that day and not talk about his futile life. She extended hand to indicate a chair in front of her, not letting go of her juice, which was quite over.

Before he sat down, Rudolph leaned forward and seemed to kiss her face. It was a gesture enough for Patricia to get out of a kind of trance that had begun just after her search for a place to sit. She was back on that Thursday morning, still warm and sunny. Now, she clearly saw Rudolph in front of her, flipping through one of his books. She ventured to ask:

- Did you see Milena today?

- Yep, I saw her. We chatted a bit outside the library for a long time. - He spoke without turning his gaze to her.

After a few moments she asked:

- And how is she? - She raised a note of concern in the voice.

- She's fine! - He looked at Patricia and continued.

- If you continue to quarrel with us, the only real friends to you in this world, you will end up as lonely as that statue there. He pointed his nose at a statue of a Greek nymph that represented autumn, something a little sad and introspective.

Before the spontaneity of Rudolph and with his ability to synthesize the facts, ironizing her recent behavior, she blushed the face while she opened a shy smile. This time she looked right into Rudolph's eyes as if apologizing to him as well. And she said to him:

- Thank you Rudolph, but... I'm going through such a difficult time in my life... Yesterday I had a kind of migraine, and...

- I know everything, do not worry. Go to the library and talk to Milena. She deserves it. - He turned to his book.

Patricia took one last sip of her juice and realized how sweet it was! *"- My God! I'll be hyperglycemic for two days!"* - She laughed at herself as she took the notebook and went to the library. She said goodbye to Rudolph and went for reconciliation with Milena.

Rudolph sat still, and no one would bother him there. He was oblivious to what others could say or speak. His abilities were far beyond what ordinary people could even understand. And helping Patricia was one of his ambitions. Milena in the second, first is Patricia. *"She is the one who needed greater and better care."* - He concluded.

3rd Week

Every hour those days passed without color or taste. Just a useless accumulation of time and tasks that made Patricia's life experience a little bit heavy. For most of them, who could observe that girl walking and relating, they could present a true physical-psychic picture of stress. But very deep in her soul, some shadows were projected over almost everything. For the trees, only the sight is the driest and twisted. The flowers only withered. If water, it's just dirty and polluted. Clouds carried the sun away and the wind can always bring on the bad smells.

But soon after they reconciled, Milena began a more intense process of helping her friend with several fronts. She was noticing some of the changes in Patricia's mood and especially her behavior, which were not pleasing to her: absence of makeup; continuous use of the same style of clothing; hair not being well combed for months. Not that she should be an example of vanity, but she was definitely losing the ability, or rather the interest in caring for herself.

Another task for Milena was related to Patricia's social interactions. She had noticed that she only left by herself. Even with the company of her two friends, she, more present, and Rudolph eventually, it was very frequent to see her alone. She had no news of meetings, lunches, or any other kind of schedule that could be considered a social activity.

But for this, she should start with another activity front: try to insert Patricia in social networks! She simply did not exist in the virtual world, too.

First of all, her cellphone was archaic and limited. Not that she couldn't buy a better one, but in short, she was not in the habit of interacting with people, also on the internet.

As always, Milena contacted Rudolph about the current situation of Patricia. Describing the facts, she considered this possibility of improvement of the mental pictures of her, through positive social interactions. Rudolph listened patiently, then nodded. *"- Yes, it was a good chance for Patrícia's mood to improve.";* "*- But watch out for the risks!*" – He´s pondering as well.

The morning after, Saturday, they went to a department store to buy clothes, makeup and a beautiful smartphone, and then Patricia would leave the twentieth century and definitely enter the twentieth one century.

It was a hard struggle for Patricia's agreement for those questions. The facts and arguments were against Milena, until she insinuated Patricia had a kind of public phobia. Those words echoed briefly in Patricia's mind, she grimaced and said,

- Of course not! Why are you pointing your finger on me? - She said, blushing.

- I don´t know Paty, you´re afraid to speak in public, you do not present group work... I've never seen you producing for class, sitting back halfway! - She spoke while enumerated with the fingers of her right hand.

- Ridiculous! Just ridiculous this conclusion! - With her backs against the wall.

- Then prove me wrong and go to the store, at least to get a cellphone for you! - If your father calls you, at least you can get a cellphone that works. - She said between a restrained laugh.

That was enough! They looked at each other for a few seconds and it was enough for Patricia to be convinced to buy a new cell phone. Her father had difficulty speaking to her on the old device, he just did not call her for months! But what if an accident with her father could happen? She couldn't rely on a device that ended the battery in minutes and was having signal problems. The time is up!

On that day, exclusively, to go to the store, wearing a bit more fancy than usual, but far from an ideal for a girl of almost twenty years. New socks, new pants and a knit sweater are more colorful than usual. It was ready, until Milena approached and looking at her and said:

- Wait a minute!

She noticed that her friend was in need of lipstick. She pointed to Patricia's face and toward her mouth, made a horizontal gesture with her index finger. Patricia was almost confused, when she remembered this woman's first-aid item. She went to her purse and took a lipstick from the bottom and began to pass.

- Wow! What is it? - She gave a little grimace when she saw herself in the mirror.

- It's lipstick, you fool! - Milena said, trying to keep a serious expression as Patricia saw the result.

- I don't need that, you know! - She looked at the lipstick near her mouth like a burning candle.

Milena positioned herself behind Patricia in the mirror and said.

- Patricia, when we are in the world today, there are things we cannot afford to do. As a great chance, we should enjoy the moments in which we are alive to learn something new. And when we already know, things kept in our consciousness as right and good, we should always put them into practice, avoiding the stagnation and decade. For example: personal care! They are a small key to relationships with people in this world! As much as we can think of avoiding diseases, mental states of well-being and personal hygiene are a door to coexistence and love, did you got that?! Whoever does not love yourself, who does not take care of yourself, certainly will not do it with someone else. This brief speech of Milena was heard in silence by Patricia.

Milena said no more. The operation was complete, and Patricia gained a new air with her mouth marked by that lipstick. It was not specifically her tone, but it was a good start to try to improve her mood with a touch of vanity and self-esteem.

They entered the store together, for Milena a tranquil and desired scene. But for Patricia a confusion of colors, smells and people who looked at her and possibly censored her by the flashy appearance. She was feeling bad, sometimes chilling, or rather sweating. With each section, step or approach of a salesperson, she thought she would vomit right there. Her head was spinning and her hands were sweating cold. *"It was something I ate..."* - She thought.

For a few moments, she thought she was lost from Milena. She imagined her friend was on her side, but she turned in another section on the left to a quieter spot in the store, where Milena was no longer at her sight. There, she was quite alone, just like a pass of magic. After all, she needed it most that moment. The deafening noise of people laughing, speaking and buying was distant and she could finally hear the store's ambient sound system, which played Nat King Cole: Unforgettable, at least it seemed to be. She was frightened when a middle-aged gentleman in the shop came to meet her and asked:

- Do you feel alright, don´t you? - He spoke serenely and solemnly.

- Yes ... I do think so ... - Scared.

- If you want to stay here any longer, just talk? - He spoke while looking around.

- No thanks... I need to find my friend!

- Where she is now, she cannot help you, but if you want, I can take you back. - He said, looking at the way out.

Patricia saw something nice and familiar in that gentleman who wore a different uniform with a perfume that her father used when she was a child ... "*What place was that!?*" It looked like a store from the 1980´s. I had not noticed that the decor in that atmosphere was outdated and poorly maintained. She took courage and said:

- I want to get out of here. - Staring at the gentleman who continued his calm face.

He lowered his head in obedience and indicated with his left arm the way back to the other section of the store she wanted to be. Patricia was walking down two aisles that she had not noticed that they had been there before, and the noise of the store was increasing, returning to the intensity and colors of before. She arrived quickly where she had missed Milena, who was distressed for the moments, to be with her friend instead. She was looking at new printers when Patricia appeared at her side. With her color turned to white and dizzier than before.

Milena said nothing until they reached the electronics section and asked her to sit down.

- Why do you wanna me to sit down? - She said putting her hands on her waist, but:

- Yes... I do not feel very well... - She spoke in a low voice, so that only Milena could hear.

Milena, annoyed but at the same time worried, indicated a couch that was on the opposite wall. Patricia speaks to her:

- I'll choose one after it gets better. - And they went straight to the couch.

Milena stood there waiting for her friend, like a loyalty dog. Worried about her friend's skin tone. She'd never seen her friend like this before, and felt guilty for exposing her like that. She just reached one of her boundaries. However, she was very intrigued by the fact that they lost themselves like that. I believed that they had a very strong tune, so that it would not be possible to speak at any moment, even briefly. "*What would have happened to her?*" - She thought.

The purchase was so quick, but the state of Patricia did not improve. So much that they had to return by taxi to the boarding house. On the way Patricia just stared out the window and cried.

Milena held her hand and tried to diagnose her friend from a clinical point of view.

- How does it feel? - Assumed a more medical position than a friend at that time.

- I have chills ... and a desire to cry! - Said Patricia with great difficulty.

Milena tried to take her wrist and looked at her iris. Then she asked Patricia to try to lay her head on her lap. So they went to the right address.

The taxi driver did not fit much, except the old judgment oriented for years at work: "*Party time! I can smell it miles away... I bet there was a man in between.*" - He thought that mechanically, seeing in the rear view mirror, the girl was now laying in the back seat of her cab."

Arriving there, Patricia went straight to the bathroom to vomit, she was pale as a dish. Milena went behind to try to hold her head. She laid her down on the bed and placed her new toy next to her. She told her:

- Are you going to get some food? - As if she already knew the answer. - She turned back and left Patricia recovering.

4Th Week

- You might have to join some social network! - Milena insisted.

- But for what? If I never needed to be in one of those! - Replied Patricia, accompanied by a reproachful look on Rudolph.

They're going down in the corridor, and Milena again:

- You have not invested a small fortune in a next generation cell phone to simply go offline!

- Get on it, Patricia! There's a world out there waiting for you! - She spoke dramatically to try to convince her.

- But Milena, I have my study schedules, my privacy... How can I keep these things I like best? - Almost complying.

- Paty, at least you have someone to talk to when your dad doesn't call you." - She spoke as Rudolph nodded.

- Ok... But you help me to register, I do not understand anything about those things! She spoke in a blend of curiosity and fatigue.

They entered the classroom, already with the schedule for a meeting and finally, they would be able to put the register of Patricia in a social network. They've agreed after class to gather in their traditional pub and only leave soon after that task.

The class passed in a normal tune, on the other hand, monotonous. In fact they were more interested in leaving after class than paying attention in the last hour of that Thursday's class.

Arriving at the pub, they saw that their favorite table was occupied, so they went to another, with the same characteristics, four chairs, leaning against the wall and near the bathroom. In fact, it was the table in the corner opposite their favorite one. As if it was reflected in a mirror.

She was able to order her traditional beer, but Patricia unexpectedly changed her mind and ordered a glass of water! Everyone looked at her after the unusual request:

- What happened to you?! - Rudolph spoke, with a face to which he spoke to a stranger.

- I'm not in the mood for a drink today. - Patricia said, looking at the cellphone in her hands.

Rudolph sought the look of Milena, who shrugged to acknowledge Rudolph's surprise. Something did not seem to make sense.

After the first sip of Patricia, Milena began her speech's geek about the internet and social networks. Very qualified for the one who accompanied a nursing course. Rudolph listened to Milena's enthusiastic narrative, now acknowledging, now reporting on facts and dates that Milena knew best.

With the cellphone in the hands of her friend, she switched from cyberspace to hardware orientation to start talking about the mobile phone and its features.

After they got the Wi-Fi signal from the pub they were in. Milena guided Patricia, who started surfing for Facebook©. All college students joined this network. Except Patricia, of course. So it should be the first social network to bring the young university student to the virtual world. They started by choosing the access name, nothing too complex, since the options were restricted: "Patricia Chase." So, they needed a photo. Milena said:

- Patricia, get up and stand there by the light so her face lights up. - She pointed to a corner where there was a bright beer sign. Then ask the waiter to take a picture of you.

With some laziness, Patricia stood up and positioned herself under the sign. But the light, even weak, bothered her.

The waiter, understanding what she wanted, came up to her and asked,

- May I help you?

- Yes, you can! Take a picture of me, please? - She spoke in a louder voice.

The waiter directed the cellphone to her and... Nothing! He had not turned on the flash, but still something must have come out of the camera's powerful lens. The photo went completely dark. Not even a point of light of the luminous left. The waiter thought it odd and he whined. He had a new idea of placing Patricia near the balcony, where there was a mirror. It would be a more conceptual picture with reflexes, almost a selfie.

Patricia with more contrariety positioned itself in the new indicated place. Her face would not be more serious than the one she was demonstrating under the red light of the balcony light. A mixture of anger, sadness and shame to be standing there for all to see. "*Who was that crazy there ?!*" I thought as I waited for the waiter to find the best angle for the photo.

The pub windows were closed and there was a heat in the middle of the night. She'd be too clothed for the interests of some insinuating pretender, yet she was cold. "*How can I think of the cold?*" During the ten seconds that the waiter's posture choices lasted, she just shivered.

She felt helpless and ridiculous in that situation. There came the smell of the nearby bathrooms, filling her noose, remembering that we are humans and animals. There came the silence of the people thinking weird things in the midst of the room. She paused to remember that there must be peace someplace dark and secure. The one that none would dare try to discover or devastate. She wanted to be at the bottom of a cave now, just listening to his breath. Or maybe not even that...

The waiter did not give up on seeing that his second attempt had resulted in a colorful blur. He went to the setup of the device to find out why he could not do such a simple operation.

Patricia had already given up when the waiter ask:

- Calm down, I've figured it out! Please go back there.

- Enough for me! Patricia said quietly. - But with the approach of Rudolph who replaced her in the position smiling she let herself be taken to a new section of photos.

This time it was easier, but she decided to take 4 photos to ensure and for the girl to choose after which was the best. He just wanted to keep his own reputation as a good small pub photographer.

As the waiter took the pictures and asked for smiles and poses, Patricia was assaulted again by that bad feeling. *"I wanted to run away from here!"* – *"I´m about to cry…"* – *"I want to feel pain …"* It seemed that there was a cold that burned inside and a feeling that there were no walls in that place. Just a spotlight above her head. Her stomach ached and the head was spinning. She was just about to faint with the eternity that presented itself to her. This all lasted until the waiter passed and told her,

- Here's your cell phone. - He said a little embarrassed over his inefficiency.

Patricia just raised her arm with no look, not out of spite, but it was the most she could do at that moment.

That's when Milena finally came and told her to be returned to the table.

- One day these feelings will pass! - Have faith.

Then she turned and went to the balcony. Patricia was startled by this presence and her intrusion. *"How dare she knows my condition?"*

She turned to her place, even before the waiter turn his face over, *"I wanted some water!"* She wanted peace and wanted to get out of there as soon as possible.

Milena returned to the table, began to see the result of the photos while Patricia ran her finger on the screen. The first one went dark. The second came out with Patricia's face erased. The third one left with her face turned and a reddish stain at her side, distorting the reflection of the mirror and the fourth, caught Patricia in motion.

Milena, in a mixture of disappointment and confidence, helped the friend to begin filling the register. She was silent, drinking the water. When Rudolph returned from some hidden place. - He always did that - A moment here and the other he was there and in the blink of an eye. This time he disappeared, at all! It was like he was talking to five people at the same time, having to attend to them. By now, he would return apologetically. Sometimes he simply returns. The most interesting of this was that Patricia always heard from him important conclusions, even though he was "out" for minutes. It seemed that he was not disconnected from her or her subjects. She liked Rudolph's company, despite the restrictions.

When it came to personal data, Patricia was posting things Milena answered. She wanted her friend to put things that would make her more attractive to any virtual friends.

- Relationship status...

- Do not put anything in! *"Single looking men."* - She pointed her finger at Milena.

- Movies?... I do not like romance movies! – Answered Patricia.

- Titanic!

- Wow! It was the expression of disaster when people love each other, for me.

- A phrase you like?

- *Dieu et mon droit*!

Milena wanted her friend to post "*Loving if you learn to love...*" But up until now, she respected her intention.

- Ready! Now go on and call some of your classmates as your first friends. - Milena insisted.

- That, just a few more minutes... Ok! Welcome to the virtual world Patricia! She spoke with a smile on her face.

She paid the bill and they went to the boarding house, it was late and the other day had already begun.

Monday began as if Friday had not finished yet and the news in that mid-morning news program was not very interesting for those who were thirsty for life. Patricia didn´t realize, but she was saddened by the air catastrophes, strikes, police reports among other topics morbid in their essence.

That morning she laid on the bed between a glance at the TV and a glance at her new roommate: the new cellphone. Especially your personal page on the social network that had not received any confirmation of acceptance of your two invitations sent. She laughed a little with her photo posted at the pub. Actually, her picture just didn't look well. There was nothing but hundred percent Patricia in that pose and place. But what did Milena say to her? "*For while!*"

She had opened the settings page of your page to try to make a change. "*But why didn't I like this picture?*" She asked quietly as she zoomed out to see her face, details and expressions. "*I look so old!*" But it was not exactly what she saw in herself that left her unsatisfied, it was what she saw around her.

When she enlarged the photo further, she could see the beer marks in the pub, the colors of the lights reflected in the mirror and the reddish stain next to it. The screen resolution of her cellphone was very sharp, but even so, the stain didn't look like anything that might be familiar. She looked closely, pulled her arm away, looked more brightly... Nothing lets her got the clearance focusing on such an optical illusion.

Then suddenly, as if in a snap, she heard her name spoken in a distant metallic voice; almost imperceptible if it were unfamiliar to her. She dropped the phone with fright! For a moment afterward, look for it with eagerness and look again for the photo. Yes! It was someone!... It looked like a person coming towards her, but at the same time the mirror reflection sought to distort. It looked like a middle-aged man, it looked like her father! She did not remember anyone approaching her, at least during the photos. Just a slight discomfort, which, coincidentally began to be, not just remembered, as creeping right now. The same cold that had burned her inside and the feeling that there would be no walls with her stomach that started to hurt ... *"My God!"* These words never seemed so ordinary and empty, to the point of representing a social convention of contrariety. Nothing that would lead her at that moment to a firm believing or unshakable faith that could rely or support her at that moment. She saw even more clearly a face with the cold expression of death and a look that presented it with the emptiness of a dead body. However, this same look insisted on looking at it through the reflection of the mirror, as if it already knew that it would be sought and corresponded at that moment.

Her head fell from the pillow and the cell phone dropped from her hand to the floor! It was eleven o'clock AM, and she had definitely lost her appetite, the desire to leave, and maybe the will to live that whole day yet. For some of them, it's just *"Monday"*. For Patricia, a nefarious day of frustration and disappointment ahead.

It was a quarter past three PM when Milena arrived. They were already in college and asked Patricia about her new social network. She did not answer anything. She just kept sat quietly looking at her book while Milena sat down beside her. She knew how to respect her moments of introspection, as if she knew her thoughts, too. But she was getting annoyed more and more, Patricia was increasingly distant in those moments, and she stayed even longer, turning into black hole, every time she was taken by guilt and sadness.

Suddenly, she remembered a case that Patricia had once told her. It was not long ago, but she turned eleven years old and prepared to build her own kid house. The night before, she and her father had a little discussion about the cleaning up of her bedroom and he told her, "*When you have your own house, you can do whatever you want!*" These words marked the frequency of Patricia's thinking about its independence and autonomy. From that age, she would think of being free from her father's tutelage in some way. The next morning she gathered boxes and more cardboard boxes and a few pieces of wood to build what she thought was a "*new house*" for herself. In the backyard of her house, she began to pile up materials and personal belongings. At the end of the morning, it seemed like a pretty room, but for the appearance of a hut. While Patricia has described this story to her, she can clearly see the image of her organizing her "new home." And much more, she felt a kind of hurt and resentment were already set in her heart by tying her walls and painting fictional windows inside her work. But in the middle of the afternoon a great storm fell upon his city. And it transformed Patricia's dreams of freedom into a heap of scraps of cardboard boxes. Her dolls wet, her clothes wet, her notebooks wet, and none of what she put inside resisted the merciless weather. Maybe there was some lesson for her there, about rebellion and security. But like her little hut, her heart was temporarily lifted with unsound sensations that made her more susceptible to external changes than to internal "good weather". Milena has news and knows how to work.

Her new cellphone rang a dozen times until her friend answered as if she had just woken up in the morning.

- Hello...

- Oh Patricia! What voice is that? - A classmate on the other side.

- The only one I have!...

- It's the right person at the wrong time! - She replied, trying to be friendly.

- What do you want? - Said Patricia, already trying to sit down better.

- Do you come to class today, don´t you? Today we will have a speech early!

- Wow! I completely forgot ... What time is it?

- It's almost four o'clock PM, the lecture starts at five PM. There's still time for you to get here! She spoke with enthusiasm.

- Do not worry about me anymore, I'm already here in college. - She said goodbye.

After turning off the cellphone, Patricia regretted she had forgotten about that afternoon's event, as well as missing lunchtime, among other glitches of that day that had not yet ended.

But especially about lunch, she thought weird a fact that morning. She was not hungry the reason why she chose just one glass of juice for lunch. With the pains in her belly and the bad feeling as if she had vomited just early in the morning, she woke up with one. "*Strange smell of vomit in the room!*" But when she just set her feet on the floor that morning, she realized that she had set them on her own vomit. There was a puddle of dark, brown, sticky, smelly substance on which her two feet were stepping! She screamed trying to hold the sound with her hand flat on her mouth! "What's that?!" She slipped to the other side of the bed with difficulty, thinking, "*How did I do it!... I can't remember...*"

She ran to the bathroom to wash her face and mouth that were still dirty. And thought about cleaning up that mess before to take a shower. "*How I had vomited so much! If I had not eaten anything all day!* " Half of her bedroom was covered by this weird dark substance.

While she's taking her bath, she let the hot water comfort her aches and doubts about that afternoon. She packed her things and picked up her cellphone. She made sure she did not delete the photo from her personal page, and then she could show it to Milena and Rudolph. They could certainly help her. "*I need help ...*" She repeated this to herself as she closed her door with keys and headed toward college, leaving the mess closed behind. But the hunger of the body was now a mere detail.

She went straight to the auditorium to attend the lecture. She entered a small line, when he saw Milena again, and Rudolph more distant. She did not want to talk to them at the time, but because of Milena's insistence, she began a little conversation with them, while the line did not move.

- Hello Paty, how nice you got here in time! - Milena said.

- Hi Paty! - Rudolph moved to his face for a kiss on the cheek. - How are you?

- Ah... Yes... Not very well as you can see! Actually, she was the one who wanted to answer that question differently.

- Yes I understand. But why are you showing us a bad look today? He spoke in a friendly tone.

- I did not sleep well tonight, that's all!" - Patricia said, summing up a little of their concern.

Yes, the appearance of Patricia really was not good. Her face looked ten years older, with dark circles and wrinkles of expression. She looked downcast with less light in her eyes as usual. Her friends, or future health workers, began a series of questions about her last hours to see how Patricia came here today looking like a patient. That Patricia tried to respond amidst laughter and innuendo of the other people in line who laughed at this "weird dialogue" revealed.

They entered the lecture and sat together in the same row, a little further behind to exchange impressions and laughter. - Patricia said as she sat down:

- I need to talk to you! - She spoke quietly to Milena.

- What's it?! - Milena said worriedly in a whispering voice.

- It's about Facebook...

- Yeah, what's wrong? - Milena was worried and curious.

- I can't talk now... After the lecture I'll tell you.

- Hush! - Rudolph did in reprisal for that dialogue. It was more of a concern to throw

Patricia into a new tangle of worries, than to be disturbing the boring lecture.

A little far from here, Giselle, who had called that afternoon, was glad for Patricia to come.

Soon after, in the exit corridor, Patricia hurriedly showed her impressions of her photo, but no matter how she showed where the mysterious face was, both Milena and Rudolph saw nothing. Only she was able to detail where that was and what was the expression of a supposed face on that photo. Even with insistence, they both always shook their heads off. Until they looked at each other and had a silent conclusion that Patricia, her sweet and reclusive friend was on the verge of a nervous breakdown and needed their help very much.

Milena was the first to lie, so Patricia would not scream desperately in the corridor. Going crazy, only she could see the silhouette with a morbid smile. Rudolph also entered the climate of the palliative solution and declared now that he was seeing. It worked! Patricia calmed down and began to shed a tear, remembering the sensations and emotions of that afternoon. "*Yes, I'm not crazy!*" She thought to herself.

She just could not keep up with the laughter of two students who passed in the corridor while she held the cellphone and swayed in disgust at the denial of her two friends. For those, she really would be crazy.

Milena asked her not to delete the picture or cancel her account on the social network. She had plans for Patricia's life to improve from the interactions, and was very interested in providing. She had a plan in mind and Patricia would be the main beneficiary. Even though she didn't know that several people also wanted to have Patricia as beneficiary, they just have a lack of means.

6th Week

That Tuesday Patricia woke up a little more willing, although still slightly behind schedule. She got up and went to the bathroom, but before she got the cellphone to see what time it was. *"Wow! It's nine and half o'clock AM! Warning!!"*.

She needed to be in college that day exceptionally at two o'clock PM for a parasitology test and still needed to study some more. She thought to herself, *"I'll have something to eat later!"*

Then she needed to run to the library at least thirty past ten o´clock AM. Otherwise, she would not take advantage of the morning time. It seemed like nothing was set for her. Short delays, deadlines, and expiration dates... it was as if she was losing some of the real-time notion, or simply failing to keep her performance as well. Tiredness, stress, anguish, everything seemed to swell with the approaching of the test time.

She left the place with the cellphone on if she needed to contact anyone, or if she got a message by the way. She was beginning to create a bond of need with that device, but much more stimulated by Milena´s asking than by necessity of use. There are the people, not an object itself.

In the meantime, waiting for Patricia's arrival, Milena took the opportunity to encourage a group of Patricia's colleagues to add her friend so that she could increase her social reach and interact with more people. Rudolph did the same as he wandered the corridors of college. For almost thirty minutes, he was mentally choosing one or the other and getting close, asked to invite Patricia Chase to be a virtual friend.

- Ready! - Rudolph said. - I've already contacted everyone! Too bad there are a lot of lady killers around here... Laughs.

- I finished it, too! I hope the recently called "friends" do their part and save Paty from ostracism.

- Why don't you speak English every now and then? - Rudolph spoke concerned about the meaning of that word.

- Rudolph, it sounds no good to be a doctor of souls, or even a future doctor in the service of God, not to have mastery of English, or the cultured standard of language. So you have to strive, and read more. - Milena spoke with some patience over her years old.

Rudolph simply nodded and went back to the books in front of. It was just what he needed to know at that stage of her life. Milena, in turn, should be able just to follow up patients. A medicine for healing and recovery of sick people. No Latin, Greek or Aramaic... He was happier with himself, than with Milena's anger.

On the way to the college, Patricia's cell phone rang for a notification. It was Giselle asking in Messenger® if she was near bound. She said yes, it was just two more blocks to the main gate.

Reaching the library, she greeted her friends along with an apology and placed her material on the table, including her cellphone. When Milena saw it, she could not contain herself and asked:

-Paty, did you get any invitation to be a friend of someone? - She spoke trying to sound natural.

Rudolph looked at her curiously for the answer, for he was also involved in the little plan.

- As far as I can see, no... How do I check this out?

Milena quickly insisted that Patricia look on her cellphone, but seeing that she was password-protected she hoped she would unlock it in a strange expectation that linked technology and emotion. When she opened it, she went straight to the network application and started real stalking.

"*Nothing yet...*" - She placed the disappointed cell phone on the table, the result was null.

- When it's evening, then class, let's look again. OK? - Patricia said sadly.

Without understanding why she was so worried about her two friends, Patricia finally sat down to study. It was very content though I needed to review it! She began to study, until Milena asked Patricia to pay attention to a book she had taken out last week. Patricia searched among those that were there, but remembered that she had returned it last Friday. She said determined:

- Do not worry, I'll go there and pick you up again. - She commented.

- I think it'll be the key to the test. - Milena said smiling.

Patricia looked into her eyes, realized the emphasis she gave with that look on her words.

She stood up determined.

She knew which bookcase the book was, but along the way, something caught her attention in the second corridor. A young lady, maybe a novice, had a book open in her hands, but she was staring at her, as if she knew her and expected to acknowledge her, maybe nodding to her, something like that. She averted her gaze as she stared into those light brown eyes that did not express much of anything but coldness.

She continued her journey to the "H" shelf and on the shelf two hundred four below would be the copies... She is again! Stranger passed by her now, but this student was posted in the same position holding a book to look at it in the same way. She felt a chill as she stared back at those distant, deep-set eyes! She ran her hands over her arms in an attempt to warm herself up or make that shiver go away. But it was as if she had no more skin sense. She did not feel her hands or arms, she knew instinctively that she was moving her arms along the opposing forearms, but she could not feel the movement. For a moment she tried to say something and greet the girl, but the words did not come out of mouth, indeed, not even the phrases formed in her mind. Just the intention.

The girl did not say anything. Just brought the index finger to her lips and made a traditional signal of silence. Just like the one ever common in a library. But, what was the sound of fear? Patricia was petrified before an unknown person who inspired her panic. Why? She looked beautiful, she looked young... She tried in vain to move her legs for a few more meters... She was on the "G" shelf, more inches to look away from her and go to her goal. "*My God*! *I want to get out of here*! She thought as she tried to pull her feet off the ground.

For a few seconds, in her perception, she turned her gaze to the "H" bookshelf and when she turned around the girl was no longer in the original position. It was inches from your body! Crossed a distance of five meters in a fraction of a second... "*What*!" Patricia's head now ached and swung in front of the young woman.

The novice woman stretched out her arm and tried to run her hand through the tips of Patricia's hair that had a mixture of aversion and tenderness in that intimate gesture. But when the other student opened her mouth, a sickly smell of meat and feces entered her nostrils making her almost vomit. At that very moment, she saw a clear tear appear in the corner of the right eye of the young woman who now seemed to have a very sad expression. The tear began to roll down her pale face, but it grew darker as she came down, even dripping to the ground in a purple splash! This scene passed Patricia slowly, to the point that she felt the pain of a cut in her wrists. This pain lasted until she felt the vibration of his cellphone in his pocket.

Her distraction, with the effect of the vibration around her body caused, the turn her head down and look for this device that insisted on vibrating.

When she pressed it to her ear, she was alone!

- Paty, where are you darling? - It was her aunt who worried about the misinformation about her.

- Oh... Who... I'm still here... - She spoke as she tried to regain her senses.

- You´ve gone away since last year! – Are you alive?

- Yes I am! - No patience to answer.

Her aunt began a planned sequence of subjects and questions for which he already had answers, especially those related to the health of her brother, father of Patricia.

In the middle of the conversation, Milena came to her side pointing her finger over an imaginary clock on her wrist.

- We're late.

She was half embarrassed by the unexpected call, went through the subject and apologized, as she was going to take a test at that very moment. The aunt still complained about her lack of attention until she hung up. She looked at the call time that marked three minutes of monologue. A new record to her aunt Heidi, her father's younger nosy sister.

But the time that caught her attention was the quest for that book. It had been fifteen minutes since she had left the table in search of her book, and the girl had vanished as if in magic. She looked at the floor to see if there was a dark stain ... Nothing!

7th Week

After that week of testing, Patricia spent the days more calmly and can even work out a little. She was thin, but out of shape. That's why, fifteen minutes walking left her out of breath and with severe ankles.

She returned to the boarding house to begin a routine of studies in front of the new demands of the course. *"Ohh this course! Is there life after the eighth semester?* "She thought to herself and laughed not to show a small shade of frustration with the performance.

She demanded more than she could do, and that reflected in her mood and health. Her general state of consciousness fluttered with anxiety and fragility that were sources for her insomnia and nervous anorexia.

She was get out from the shower, when her cellphone rang. It was her classmate who was already on her halfway to college and very excited.

- Paty! Good morning! How about your tests? - She asked curiously about this result expected and desired by them.

- Hello Giselle, how are you? No, I can't figure out anything. She spoke through speakerphone as she combed, regretting once more that she had given her cellphone number to her.

- Oh silly girl?! – Can you be sure of a great result, can´t you?!

- Why be sure at all? - Patricia retorted.

- Why? -You are young, beautiful and intelligent and don't care at all! - tried to disguise her interest in proving that it would be the best of the class, in case Patricia indicated that its results would not be of the best.

Certainly, no one in her class, apart from her two closest friends, knew that her great frustration was even Medicine, but afraid of having another failure in life, ended up opting for Nursing at the time of choosing the college degree. For her distant relatives, not just physically, she was doing medicine. White clothes, books, materials, early classes and the atmosphere of the course were apparently similar. Except for the gender of the students, likely there are more profile females in the course.

In this scenario of competition and conflict, Patricia became even more distant and little averse to easy laughter. She pushed companies aside because of their natural and persistent lack of vanity, and their natural and notorious capacity for dedication. There was no female friendship to resist this competition, or male friendship to endure this sloppiness. And vice versa. Due to a need and geographical proximity, by the way, only Rudolph and Milena managed to penetrate this aura of dedication and stress called Patricia. Or was it because she allowed it?

Later, already inside Patricia's room, Milena made some expression wrinkles when she received the news of the failure of the strategy and the invitations of friends for Patricia. "*When I get to college, I'll have her pick up the cellphone and accept all the invitations, and also look for other friends for her, oh, I´m gonna do that!*" They went to college together that afternoon, sitting side by side on the bus. But it was Patricia who started a small dialogue:

- Milena, when you meet me, how do you know if I'm sad or happy? - She asked without turning to her friend.

- Patricia, I always know how you do. I can feel this from a considerable distance from you! When there is a connection between two or more people, it is almost impossible for us not to be moved when the person we like is sad or happy. We began to vibrate in a single stream.

- How is this possible? - A little more interested, but disbelieving Milena's words.

- Patricia, I as your father, and Rudolph, or even your mother, wherever she may be, all of us know about you more than you realize. We are, I believe, intertwined in a tangle of lives and souls. She said this in a didactic tone, as if he already mastered the subject and was adapting to her friend's understanding.

Patricia glanced in her direction at the hands that gestured with intent to teach for a few moments and then said:

- Milena, you've known me for a long time. I really do not know much about you. All I know is that it's good to be with you. But when you talk about certain subjects, I think there's something you want to show me. Such a world that I don´t know best. So, who are you trying to tell me something like that? You are as young as I am, or come from the small town, full of dreams and problems. Do not tell me, please, these subjects about metaphysics or esoteric stuff. She turned to the bus window.

- But you started the question, not me.

- Yes, I said that because I wanted a more objective and palpable response, nor faking or charlatanism ideas.

- But you'd like the answers. The ones you just figure out the real world. - Would life be so easy?

- Milena, you should at least respect my boundaries and preferences. I do not like these matters of soul, or kingdom Come. OK?

During the dialog, Milena got up for a lady to sit down. She stood beside Patricia watching her face. The dialog had finished at that moment, because Patricia didn´t want to share with that lady her most intimate matters. They got off the bus together, but each went in opposite directions.

Already in college, Patricia met Rudolph who was excited in a circle of acquaintances and laughing at his cases. They gazed long enough for Rudolph to know that she was not well. In fact, Patricia seemed to lose that semblance she had noticed on the first day of class. "*Maybe something has died inside?*" He thought quickly as he smiled at her, when beckoned a hello.

She met Milena later on the couch at the lobby. And this one had a more serious face and a more worried look. Took advantage and get a vacant place nearby. Then I sat down.

- Hi Mi, what happened? - Patricia said that as she set her things down.

- Nothing, but have you looked at your cell phone again? - She used her hand to point to the device in Patricia's hand.

- Sure, what´s for? She spoke solicitously, opening the locking screen.

- I don't want you to call, I just wanna see something...

- Wow, you're making me worried. What's that?

- Your Facebook, why is it blocked? - She spoke as she searched for reasons to have had no contact so far.

- Here, I got it! My setup was locked for people who were unknown. She said that, but not for sure. It just disabled some new privacy parameters that it had not previously identified.

- Ok, from now on I'm worth it! But let me see... I'm going to invite Claudia and Priscilla from our class. They seem to be nicer than Giselle.

Patricia spoke no more, she just occupied her role to be guarded by Milena with social and technological issues. Actually, Milena had something protective and affectionate. Even though she deeply guessed Claudia and "*...what's her name again*?" Futile and unintelligent girls, she thought they would help Patricia in her network somehow.

Patricia, as proof that she was struggling to be social, as her friend would like, would accept this new effort. After all, she was very nervous about everything, about the events in the store, at the pub, and then at the library... She should be very stressed to have such variations of metabolism and humor. "*I do not feed myself also!*" She blamed herself even more as she completed her actions. Not that it whetted her appetite, but rather inhibited her desire to eat indeed.

Catching the general state of Patricia, in her form of being silent while she seems to fulfill determinations that contradict her, Milena said:

- You know Patricia, since you were a child, you told me when it was difficult for you to do your homework and duties. Clean up your room! A kind of sacrifice executed with curses and tears every time. But all of this helped you somehow. You have grown into an almost disciplined adult being. But it still has stains of its revolting past. She wanted her mother to be there to defend her father's merciless orders only screaming, but she was even more anxious that she was there to do her chores for you, or even help her a lot. Solitude or revolt? Helplessness or indolence? Your consciousness never quite managed to separate those emotions in moments of anger. But now, you are able to effect this simple commutation of thoughts. Do it yourself, do it for yourself, or if you do prefer, do it to prove to those you love that you can do some simple and trivial tasks on your own.

At the end she stopped talking and stared at Patricia silently in front of her. Those words were not said to offend her, or to diminish her, but simply to see her improving her humor.

Patricia said nothing or thought about it. She only really thought about those moments described by Milena, which were not few. She laughed as she picked up her things to go to the study room. Very intrigued by when she had told her friend about those events. Nor even many details she remembered like that.

- Shall we go to the coffee bar before the class? - She invited Milena with her slight discreet overweight.

- Oh... Why don't we wait six more hours to eat at the end of class? - Said Patricia, quite not hungry. Useless.

She had an espresso and tried to savor a snack, while Milena talked about caloric content. It was only three in the afternoon and the rest of the day would be long for two of them. But a little longer for Patricia who would receive an unusual invitation.

Many hours later, after class, they said goodbye as usual. Rudolph had more time with her. He asked Patricia to evaluate her current diet and strengthen her carbohydrates.

- Only salads and fish would not be contributing to your muscle mass, he said in a tone of concern.

- Ok, yes sir, I'm going to review this... But tomorrow! She laughed a little.

On her way back home, everything was quite normal. The same noises, the same faces, the same houses... Just noticed there were more poles with their lights off on the way. She always noticed the lights and colors of the signs, and when they stood out in the darkness, something around her would be in trouble. "*Funny, they were well lit yesterday!*" - Patricia noted.

Arriving at her place, she locked the door and got rid of her clothes, went straight to the bathroom. It was a long bath in a bathroom with a lot of water vapor. As her room was with the light off, there was a feeling that there was a smokescreen between two worlds: the lighted one, where she was and the darkness, represented by her room. Even as dark as it was, it did not stop her from getting cozy.

Curled up in the towel, Patricia "passed between these two worlds" searching for the light switch on the wall. She found it as usual, but she could not turn on the light in her room. One, two ... Four times and nothing! "*- Damn it! It burned!*" Should put her clothes in the dark or bring your clothes to your wet bathroom.

She had an idea! She moved slowly to the bed, where her cellphone was deposited. She switched on the set so that it worked like a kind of flashlight with its screen. With that, an improvised lantern directed the focus of light to several corners of the room. And because it was filled with steam, it created an atmosphere of fog. "*Wow! I did not know that my room was so big!*" First, it was a chair that seemed occupied, but used clothes were deposited on it. Then she glanced at the bed, which looked like it was used recently, but it was the folds of the blanket that she knelt to pick up the cellphone. She played with the lights and shadows that formed, but coincidentally, it always came to mind that there were people in her room, besides herself. Every little shade projected seems even bigger and menacing her. The eyes that tried to get accustomed to the darkness were full of panic.

Before the light reached her dresser, where she kept her pajamas in the drawer, she thought had felt a person dodging the light, going to the darker side of the room. As she focused the light on the drawer, the screen went into screen rest and the lights went off! She could not measure how long she had been without light, but it was enough for her to feel colder than usual and to think more clearly that she was not alone. Now she was already listening to movements of clothes and a slight breath near, far, above or beside her, she could not tell.

When she got up with her pajamas in her hands, she placed the light beam of her cellphone in front of her vanity mirror and let out a small cry of fright when she saw a human face just behind her that hid in the darkness again as the light reflected her in the mirror. She turned the cellphone back into the darkness on the opposite side of the mirror and the beam of light illuminated her desk and a shiver ran down her spine going straight to the nape of the neck as she saw her swivel chair move slowly to the left as if something or someone had turned it, or gotten up from it. She began to tremble and to seek some sort of scientific explanation for it. Then she ran to the bathroom to change her clothes.

Already dressed and shaking, she went with the cellphone back to the switch and tried again to turn on the lights. One, two... Five times and nothing again! She remembered the lamp on her desk. She went with her cellphone to where she was and tried to turn it on. One, two ... Quickly six times! She was getting angry, or maybe desperate! *"Calm down Patricia Chase!"* She spoke to herself aloud. Thinking that they inhabited in her body two distinct entities: one in panic and the other that clung to an attempt of normality.

There was a flicker of awareness as she lowered the cellphone beam through the power cord of the lamp. Coming to the end she noticed that she was not plugged in. *"Dumb!"* She turned on the lamp and it flashes three times quickly before partially lighting every room. There was no more steam and everything seemed in its proper place. Except for the bathroom door that was now half closed.

Combining her hair, she went to the door and tried to open it for good. Her wet hand still slipped on the circular knob and the door simply did not move. She wiped the hand on her pajamas and forced the door that resisted at first as if it were being held by someone in the bath, but then gave in quickly revealing the cool, damp interior of the bathroom.

When she saw the open cupboard she remembered to brush her teeth and take her vitamins. After this operation closed the cabinet that had a mirror on its outside. How did this gesture without looking at the mirror, preferring the cellphone in his hand, didn't notice the reflection of a young and curious man as his new and young roommate. It had been by the noon he got in Patricia's room since she´d out for college. Her gaze was lost when the cell vibrated with a notification.

She opened her social networking page and there was an invitation. But a different invitation. It was Charles Burie who wanted to invite her as a friend. "Charles ... Charles ... Where do I know Charles?" But as he was supposed to be a friend of somebody in college, she ended up accepting it without first checking the personal information of this nice guest.

Ready! Patricia's network began to be built from this adhesion and her life would never be the same. Never ever.

8th Week

There were three of them talking waiting for the technical visit to the Central Hospital about to begin. Today would be a long day everyone was eager to start and end. The students of the first and third period would know the structure of the largest hospital in the city.

Several colleagues had already arrived and were grouped almost exactly as if they were in class, each group with their respective friends. However, everyone was thrilled with the much-anticipated notice by the course coordinator made several days ago.

It was a traditional visit, in a kind of agreement that the hospital maintained with the college. Not only because of this, the hospital's own chief physician has already been a student and has recently opened this possibility for the students.

You could see the motivation and the smiles on everyone's faces, who spoke aloud and laughed at the repeated and repeated situations of hospital histories. All but Milena, who listened to Patricia's narrative with an expression of astonishment and disbelief.

- Seriously, it looked like there was someone in the room with me! - She spoke convincingly.

- I don´t know... I do not think that's a very strange story about lights that cannot be turned on.

Rudolph was oblivious to this private dialogue, searching for his notes to refresh his memory, as well as photos and preparing his foray with Patricia and the others.

- Seriously Mi, it looked like someone was looking at me all the time... - Even in the shower! Now I can describe this feeling better! Oh my God, I think I´m going crazy! - She lowered her head in despair.

- Paty, you have been suffering from insecurity, loneliness, and your father's longing for some time. It is normal for our senses to be betrayed by our willingness to see something, feel something that is in our subconscious. The area of the brain responsible for the vision is the same activated by the imagination, so, even seeing real and tangible things, we can imagine more fanciful aspects about that reality that surrounds us. Where do you think our folklore came from?

- For example, today. You will be encouraged to focus on understanding, seeing new things and people. You will have to choose the messages that are going to be sent to you by doctors, nurses, and why not to tell the patients we meet. A hospital is a living and vibrant institution. Full of life and dreams. However, it may present itself as a frontier for the other world, a place of passage for many. In most cases it is a place of life, and the struggle for it. As is the case with maternity wards, they bring thousands of newborn babies to start their journey. Patricia, once inside, the only thing you will not need to use is your imagination. They are facts, data and information. But the difference between humans and the machines there is directly linked to intuition. The healing and transformation of sick souls pass through man's superior insight into understanding causes and dealing with effects. Creativity should not be confused with intuition, as in the arts. If you use it in a boundary between life and death, surely that second element will take over your will, alienating your imagination to bring it closer to that enormous force contrary to life.

Patricia still misunderstood Milena's explanation. That continued in another prism:

- You see, you do not sleep right, you eat like a little bird, I bet your blood tests would show up everything in need! You had studied more than everyone in the class in sum. You desire what? Let your body not complain! Many people present clinical pictures of stress in the most varied ways. You are tending towards paranoia apparently. - She laughed at her unscientific conclusion.

- But Milena, what if there was somebody in my room? - Am I going crazy? - She spoke it in a weaker voice.

- What a foolish creature! Shut up please! That would be a police case, that's right! But you did not say that the door was locked when you reached the room and that you had certified that it was locked when you left?

- If I locked it up when I arrived, I quite remember well, but if it was locked... I do not remember that very well. She looked down and by the left.

Milena looked up to the sky in a faint sign of impatience with Patricia's uncertainties. But she insisted:

- Paty, once and for all. Forget this episode. You are alright. Nothing really happened to you, you have this week still ahead and a delicious technical visit to do still today! She spoke as she held Patricia's hands, but inside she was very concerned about that situation.

Patricia somehow ashamed accepted Milena's suggestions and to prove she was better said:

- Ok! Oh, you know I got my first invitation from Facebook! - She spoke half proudly.

- Oh really! - Said Milena smiling with her eyes!

- Yes, you want to see, Charles, Charles... She tried to remember his surname while she searched her cell for proof of her affirmation.

- Oh here! Burie. - Do you know him?

Milena placed her hand over the shell-shaped screen to dim the reflection.

- No, I don´t know him. He was not the one that I... I mean, it's not part of my network. Did you look at his data?

- Of course not! I thought you were friends with somebody here in college. - He looked so good in this photo...

- You're really crazy! - Milena said, after a brief moment watching Patricia smile. - How do you accept someone "*inside your home*" without knowing him for sure! She used that tone, also in reference to what her friend had told her now, about the episode of the sensation of invasion. In her speech and intentions, she wanted to use Patricia's negative feelings in favor of her, to raise her precaution, even in the virtual world.

- Wow! I made a stupid move... - How do you delete it? - Milena instructed her, then she picked up her cellphone and started rummaging through the data before dismissing the contact.

- *Charles J. Burie, born in 1975... hamm, older!... Let me see... photos... nothing yet... films... known persons: 1.276 Wow... Popular! None in common... Works with sales... Widow!* - Milena listened to this story and thought at the same time. When Patricia finally positioned herself to exclude the contact, there was the call to enter the hospital. She immediately put away the cellphone, without having completed her task. Charles was still her friend. He went with her into the hospital, why not meant to say, inside of her life.

The visit was pleasant for all of them. Photos, selfies, notes, audios and filming all were collecting the largest volume of data possible with their mobile handsets. Including Patricia who was surrendering to the technology possibilities provided by her new mobile device.

They went to the kitchen of the hospital, to the laundry, to the management room, to the drug center... This first "uninteresting" part for a nursing student was done first. They followed with curiosity, but without many questions, or enthusiasm. Until the lunch break, it was made in the staff restaurant along with some doctors and nurses.

They wanted to sit together, but it was not possible. So Patricia turned her backs on Rudolph and Milena, who were able to sit side by side. But that was no obstacle to talk to each other. Since they turned or spoke in a higher tone, favoring the dialogue at a distance.

Milena and Rudolph sat in the direction of an immense pane of glass that led to the back of the hospital, while Patricia headed toward the entrance to the refectory, from which she could see almost everyone. As they talked, one fact caught Patricia's attention. It was a young woman who was holding her tray with her meal standing, looking for a place to sit. Even with some places still available near her, she seemed to want to find a specific person or place. Until she looked at her! The young doctor stared at Patricia with a sight, cold and distant. No facial expression of warmth or familiarity. She began to walk slowly toward Patricia, not looking at her tray or path, just coming and walking in short steps. People got up and she did not sit anywhere. So much so that Patricia looked sideways to see if there was an empty space around her, that the young doctor would be interested in sitting down, but everyone was busy. With every step the woman took in her direction, the noise of the room, as the voices of the guests were lowered, so the silence grew around Patricia as she approached. Even she cannot hear anything but her own panting. When she looked up, the young woman doctor was already halfway away from her and could see her face more clearly.

Without noticing on their plate, the vegetables were dehydrating and drying. Darkening with every step the doctor gave toward her. She stared at her and the steak on the plate went darkening and rapidly decomposing.

In the doctor's eyes, there was an expression of calm and serenity, but at the same time there was hurt and rancor from the window of cold, half-open eyes staring at her. Her pale mouth was dry and her thin lips tightened as if she were in some pain. One more step, another... She was almost ten feet away from Patricia, who could see that there was nothing on her plate! It was dirty but empty, at least there was not enough food in the center to be higher than the edge. Patricia shook her knees in a real shivering sensation and felt her heart soar! *"Adrenaline!..."* Soon her appetite went away, and suddenly the smell of the food in front of her finally seemed sickening to her, as if she had already been chewed by somebody, almost covered still by gastric juice and with a bilious aroma of a digestion which was beginning. She vomited as she pushed her plate away!

As she tried to get her attention back to the young doctor, there was a real silence in the room that had been so noisy. In the midst of a lull of silenced voices and cutlery, she saw her five feet away still holding her tray with the empty plate, but she noticed that her jaw was discreetly moving in a circular motion from top to bottom. Slowly one, two... She would complete the third turn, when two doctors passed in front of the young doctor obstructing her eye contact with Patricia circumstantially. They passed and she followed them with a look of annoyance at having obstructed her view of the young woman doctor. As she turned her gaze back to those cold eyes, but she had simply gone! She disappeared as if in a trick of illusionism, Patricia rose abruptly, not realizing that the turbulent sound of the refectory had resumed to her eardrums, and set off in search of the young woman doctor who should have been sitting in the vicinity. There was a woman with the young doctor's complexion, and Patricia touched her lightly on the shoulder and she was startled to see a completely different face, though with her hair in the same cut and tone. Disappear!

The visit passed quietly the rest of the afternoon, but Patricia became monosyllabic. She did not tell Milena anything that could rebuke her even more. When she came to the boarding house after today's class, she would thoroughly investigate her clinical case that was beginning to bother her. *"Or would it be a psychic case?!"* The warning light was set on.

9Th Week

She was sitting at the waiting hall in a clinic. She was the next to be attended and carried her exams in hands with a distant look.

"How did I let this happen to me!" - She was blaming and rebuking her current state of health. After having a "new" nervous breakdown at the dining hall and especially after the warnings given by Milene, she decided to investigate her clinical case. After all, if she was going to be a health professional, then she would be her first and constant patient.

When she began researching her symptoms, she went first to a search site. She knew what was scientific and what could be considered "charlatanism". She wrote down on a sheet of paper, electronic addresses, data, authors and books on associations between eating disorders and psychotic pictures of paranoia and hallucinations.

There was nothing very conclusive, due to a vast list of symptoms. Well, it fit into some syndromes, sometimes in some cases... *"Nothing Conclusive"*. So she went to an endocrinologist. She would begin to mount a huge puzzle of his real physical situation, to avoid mentally speaking.

She was sitting, when her cell phone rang with a new notification. She bent down in her chair to catch it, accompanied by an elderly gentleman sitting by the right side. She smiled at him as she took the phone from her bag on the floor. He turned his gaze to the same picture you were looking at before being interrupted by the almost inaudible touch of the cell phone. It was a surprise! A new person wanted to be her friend. This time it was a woman. Sinead T. Stone. And she seemed even nice in his picture. Accepted on time! She enjoy the moment and went to see the posts of Mr. Charles and his new friend Sinead.

Patricia was intrigued by some lack of information from her new virtual friend. Nothing could be shown in his past. For example, the posts were just for this week. She was going to send a direct message to him, when the assistant called her by name.

She hurried inside with her belongings and ran onto a very young doctor who made her uncomfortable somehow. She decided not to say anything about her studies, just to generate no kind of interest.

- Good Morning! I'm Dr. Standhall. - He spoke cordially as he took the file of his new patient.

- Good Morning. She answered, hushing her voice.

- I see here that you lost your mother. What was it? He spoke without looking at her and reading the rest of the data.

- She died three months after I was born... I believe she was a... In the head or in the heart. - She decided to talk like this so as not to set the doctor's curiosity.

The doctor asked her to sit on the stretcher and take off her shoes. Meanwhile, he was reading her exam results.

She stayed there seconds that seemed hours in the near attention of a handsome man who represented part of her future. She smiled a little when she imagined the opposite situation, he sat there looking foolish and she saw his exams looking worried.

Then he said, raising his voice. You have a number of deficits in blood factors that are important to your health. It would be as if you wanted to make a recipe and did not have salt or sugar... By the way, your limits are far below for a person your age. Which suggests that you appears to be an older person with serious difficulties in absorbing food and nutrients.

Patricia stared at him and paid attention to his teaching to explain the case. "How interesting!"

- That way, you have difficulty in strengthening, recovering your breath, remembering things, feeling the taste of food... Simple things that sometimes we do not realize, but that are very important. - At that moment he approached her with both hands and lowered his eyelids.

- Hamm... Too pale! How about your eating habits?

As she tried to explain, almost justifying herself for the eating disorders, but all this without mentioning the college of nursing.

Then after he asked her to stand barefoot and sit on the stretcher, he said to her:

- Look Ms. Chase, you live alone and are more than sixteen years old, so that way you should pay more attention to your vigilance over your food discipline. You can not do all that a child does, however, if you neglect the quantity and frequency needed, you reach the danger zone of your body malfunctioning. It's useless putting a lot of corrective medicine on you, if you stick to your current habits. - Break.

- I'll ask for more tests and we'll start at your liver. Soon after that, we observe other glands that we have in our body, but for this I need you to improve your diet so that the results do not hide any problems. Not they ever exist! But we have to make sure the cause is just your poor diet. OK?

- Yes! She nodded, but before she got off the stretcher, he asked her to stand by so he could auscultate her heart. As she was in a thicker jacket, he stood up the jacket a little and her shirt also, showing her ribs in an aspect of utter thinness. The cold of the stethoscope made her shiver as he urged her to take a deeper breath.

In the middle of the attendance the secretary came in and told him that there was a call in his private number and what his decision would be? He looked at Patricia and asked her to put the shoes on and sit at the chair while he went for the call, which was important, but would come back in a few minutes. She agreed.

She was sitting in that office watching all the details. Books, photos, diplomas, embellishments... We could recognize much of the personality of a doctor through those objects. So her peace was interrupted by an unexpected cell phone call. The person's icon appeared on the screen and she was already speaking:

- Giselle! What do you want? - Speaking quickly.

- Our Patricia, an animal bit you? First, good morning and hello! - Outraged.

- No, Giselle, I'm in the middle of a consultation. - Trying to explain herself.

- Ohhh! So you decided to spy on doctors now? - She spoke in a tone of vexation.

- Is not it! I'm kind of worried about my health. We'll talk tonight.

- OK. I just called to find out how you're doing, because you're gonna do our job, right? As I was called by the other classmates to be your "collector of jobs", as we like to call the greenbelts. So I am here doing this mission. Patricia, do not let us down! - Threatening.

- Okay, do not worry-" She looked at the ceiling in relief.

- Okay. We agreed. Bye, dear. We trust you! - Kisses.

She hung up the cellphone after Giselle had hung up first. She put the cellphone against his lips, in a mixture of secrecy and disgust. "*How could I get into such a situation?*" In fact, her roommates wanted to contact, and made it clear that there was a place in the study group. But they were able to influence Patricia in her weak point: the obsession with studies. They challenged her to get an excellent job, which was gradually delegated. Her vanity cannot be avoided, in addition to Milena's requests for social integration. "*What kind of integration was this? Slavery?!*"

When she put the cellphone in her bag, it was interrupted by an older nurse who entered the office. She smelled a little of old dirty clothes and a scent mixed with human sweat that made her nauseous! "*My God, what woman is that?*" The nurse did not even look at her, went straight to a bookcase with briefcases, and stopped in front of the furniture and looked at the last shelves from above. Shoes worn with crooked heels. Shredded stockings and clothes that were once quite white. They were grayish and crumpled, as if she had only been lying or sitting for a long time. His hair, in a completely out-of-fashion cut, something from the 1940s, translated consistently sloppiness into his appearance. Everything about her was out of the office's modern, aseptic place. Yet she was there! Imposing her presence.

Dr. Standhall returned and sat down in his chair, which made Patricia immediately look at him. Collecting your last instructions. He told her:

- I'm telling you two medicines for you to take until you return with these tests. - I'd rather you do at that clinic, for the quality of the results, and for the lower price. OK?

As he signed the papers she turned to look at the intruder, and she was passing through the threshold of the door that closed silently behind her. Out of discretion, it seemed best not to ask who he was.

She received Dr. Standhall's prescription and examination papers and held out her hand toward his door. He turned the key lock once before opening the door that was locked inside. They said good-bye with a handshake and he wished her good morning and even a brief return.

From there she left worried about her state of health. Delighted at the young doctor, startled by the hours ahead and intrigued, *"How could the nurse open the door inside, after she left the doctor's office?"*

10th week

She received from Charles her first Facebook® post. Very unusual and different, she wanted her other few friends to know, but it was blocked for sharing.

> "In death we find the light, from the darkness we
> separate from the pain, from above we watch the
> sun go down and from afar we are in peace!"

Although that's dingy, it was written over a photo of the refrigerator's interior where two products of animal origin were seen. They looked like cuts of meat, one sliced and the other peperoni. They were beautiful packages, but they brought death within them, or from another perspective, the life for those who could feed on those products. The one nearest to the post's words was vibrant colors, and the other, farther away, had on its label a smiling sun. From looking and checking these details, she found that very sensitive and creative. You marked "*like*" and closed the application.

She was ready to go into her first anatomy class that semester inside the lab. The others were made in the room in the presence of Mr. Thompson, a skeleton of a 38-year-old man who had been dead for 20 years, who all said and repeated the same morbid joke: "*...I didn't graduated in nursing yet, despite all this time in college.*"

Milena and Rudolph appeared there also. They were excited by the novelty of following a practical class in a laboratory like that. But they did not laugh at jokes from beyond the grave and did not even mention folk cases about autopsies and necropsies, like everyone there.

They received dozens of instructions and road maps for their tissue collection and verification procedures of shoulder joints, the theme of today's class. They also received a sheet with recommendations regarding the use and handling of their instruments.

On the way to the stands Patricia commented to Milena that she had received her first post from her little network on Facebook®. What was received with joy by Milena.

- Wow Paty, that's cool! Share with everyone, so you start your contacts window.

- No I can´t... I've tried. But it is locked for sharing. After class I'll show you. OK? - They sat down.

The class began and the helpers along with some students went to the formal tanks to remove the parts for the procedures. They wore rubber gloves, masks and goggles, while the teacher explained some safety procedures.

They placed Milena, Giselle, Rudolph, and Patricia on a stainless steel tray, a piece of dark flesh that resembled a human shoulder with the sequence of a forearm cut to half. All this wrapped in a plastic and filled with formaldehyde.

Patricia's first impression was of curiosity. Behind her goggles with a medical mask and rubber gloves, she felt safe to pull the piece out of the plastic and start the number one procedure of the task sheet.

As soon as the scalpel touched the skin of the piece of meat, Patricia felt a stab in the left shoulder and a pain that burned her left side of the chest. At the same moment, her hand began to tremble a little, which was once sharp and firm, while drops of sweat appeared on her forehead. Even with laboratory air conditioning on.

The smell of formaldehyde and the sense of familiarity of the piece with the human figure, distorted, torn and fragile. As if it was only flesh and matter, Patricia filled her eyes with tears, but she did not know whether it was a reaction to the smell of formaldehyde, or to her new state of mind acquired in the middle of that class.

Her glasses began to blur with the gasping breath, when she was interrupted by Giselle whispering, *"- Are you ok?"* - When she saw Patricia's trembling hands and her quickening breath.

- Yes... Fine. - Recovering her conscience.

She cut deeper into the flesh, deeper than was necessary, and the scalpel got stuck for something. She slipped the fingers and it slipped out of her hand. She tried to hold it harder and only managed to move it to the sides. It seemed got a bone... The piece of meat moved in the direction of Patricia's effort and she asked the next colleague to hold her hand a little. But a new effort and she noticed something that made her even more thrilled. After the scalpel had loosened and her assistant colleague reduced the pressure to keep the piece fixed, almost abandoning the piece, then again the piece moved on with yet another incision of Patricia, however, instead of turning in the direction of the force the piece turned in the opposite direction, as if trying to avoid the blade! Patricia immediately lifted the scalpel and sought the eyes of her colleagues who stopped and turned to her, encouraging her to continue. *"Why won't they see that!?"*

She pursed the lips and continued her fictional operation to find out what it was, or what the cure would be!? More carefully and slowly, she cut and parted the rigid tissues that looked like gray, overlapping rubber sheets. The piece did not move anymore.... It just trembled to the point where Patricia felt the vibration at the tip of her scalpel. She had a little nausea and asked her next colleague to hold the meat protruding with the hemostatic forceps.

From that moment on, she no longer heard the surroundings of the laboratory, neither the smell nor sound. It was a trance established between the piece and its own body. Everything was now colorless, moot or lifeless. She touched the piece with the fingertips and no longer felt stiff and dead. It was soft and tender, as if it's just been born at that moment. It had heat and pulse. At that very moment she looked ahead and saw a female body standing beside the body parts tank. She was naked and incomplete, no head and the exact part that was on her steel tray was off too. She had formaldehyde dropping along her legs, as if he was coming out of a bath without drying, or had emerged from that tank. They formed small puddles of formaldehyde around the wrinkled feet that grew as more and more formaldehyde was accumulated. The smell was unbearable! As she touched the piece in front of her with more force, the other arm of the apparition went toward the nonexistent shoulder as if trying a strike of pain. Patricia opened her mouth in terror as she heard within her consciousness someone in a female voice saying in a whisper, "Stop!!" It was enough! She left the scalpel and ran out of the bench during a vomit that went out through the sides of her medical mask. Milena and Rudolph rushed after her and the class was suspended with everyone present looking at and laughing at the situation.

In the antechamber of the lab they were both waiting for her to leave the bathroom. Worried about two different situations.

- Our Paty is not well, hum? - Milena said.

- Yeah, she's upset with the class, is the teacher going to give her credits yet? Rudolph spoke worriedly.

- Rudolph! Do not be pragmatic at this time!

- I, pragmatic?! Why? - Curious about Milena's speech.

- You are thinking only of your purpose here!

No, I'm just being objective. I am thinking of all of us that we may not succeed with our task if she does not get her training too. This practice is part of a discipline that Patricia needs to be approved. Trying to explain, while Milena left him talking to himself and went to the bathroom to help Patricia.

Inside the bathroom Patricia was standing in front of the mirror and static. Staring at her reflection as tears streamed down her face, without her showing that she was in tears. Milena, seeing that scene, did not dare ask anything. She approached slowly as she saw that demonstration of Patricia's mental confusion and imbalance. She had never seen her so frail and helpless that way.

Patricia, on the other hand, was engaging in an intense and exhausting mental dialogue. In front of her was not a reflection of herself, as Milena was witnessing. It was another female figure who was executing Patricia for having cut and torn her with a scalpel. She uttered words of insult, threats and personal offenses that were only agreed upon by Patricia in a sign of submission and confession of guilt. Each phrase of complaint and cursing was a tear that ran from Patricia, who simply could not get out of that trance, moving away or even cutting that line with her subconscious full of remorse and guilt. Her hands gripped the sink, making the fingers twitch and red. If she had more strength, she could pluck a piece of that stone. Suddenly a scream! But it was not her, out of the image that was gone, turning the mirror to present the figure of Patricia, thin, disheveled hair, with dark circles and eyes ejected from recent sobbing. But with a new problem... The scare caused by the scream reflected in her body in a urinary incontinence. She was sad, cold, dirty with vomit, helpless and wet in her private parts and along her left leg.

Milena could not hold her friend's body before she hit her head on the floor in a faint fall.

11th Week

It was Tuesday yet, and for Patricia it looked like a Friday due to the weariness and dismay of who should have worked all week. On the other hand, there will be four days for her to strive for a minimum of academic and social performance.

Luckily, her faithful companion for those hours was the cellphone with its apps. She was already posting on her personal page, but she was embarrassed to express her real state of mind, her anguish, and her pain. Much more for her few online friendships, actually seven. But there was a page of a bakery, Charles, Sinead and four other friends added, coming from Charles´ network. And with them she was most identified and related.

There were posts about places, trips and mainly thoughts, sometimes posted by Charles, sometimes posted by Sinead. They were both common friends and had one hundred more friends in common. Charles' network of friends was more extensive than Sinead's one, but both had more than hundreds of friends, all scattered around the world! *They should certainly be very popular!*

While researching for an academic article would be represented for the final credits of an important discipline, Patricia kept herself closer with Charles who already ventured some direct messages:

- How do you do, Patricia?
- Good morning, Charles!
- I see no reason to
to have a day like this ...
- LOL. You R always so formal.
- What are you doing?
- Studying!
- Save your memories
for you!

- Never forget
who are you!

- Never been better!

- Ok, we always come back...
- Ciao !.

Those conversations with Charles, even brief, were becoming more and more frequent. In addition Milena, who kept constant dialogue with her, and the inspiring friend Rudolph. They rather were the only two "flesh and blood" people she had ever met outside of college.

Her father, so distant, called last week, but with problems of line and voice choked by emotion, generated a very vague and limited phone call. She had to hang up, as it was exhausting to raise her voice to be understood and repeatedly have to say the same sentences.

She remembered the first time she had to present a school report to her father. This emotion never had gone away. He was sitting in his favorite chair at desk. She reached behind him and slipped the school report tucked in half, hesitantly and carefully not to arouse him from the professional trance. Sensing at his elbow, the paper he had pushed quickly turned and grabbed his daughter's wrist swiftly and quickly. She tried to pull her arm out and run away, but it was in vain. Her father's strength and the sliding white socks immobilized Patricia's intention. The Father won´t let go of her hand while reading her school report. Patricia begged him to let her go. With one hand, he finished the reading and left the bulletin above his desk. Then he stared at Patricia, releasing her hand. She knew not to do anything but stand and listen. He said in a slow voice, *"If you want to be someone in your life, you'll have to stop having weak results."* Somehow she knew he was going to speak to her like that! It was not the first time he had spoken to her about this "*being someone*" situation. "*Hey! I am your daughter!*"; "*I'm a girl!*"; "*I am a student! What else should I do to be somebody?*" She picked up her signed bulletin and realized her father considered "someone, who got "A" in all school stuff and not just "B" as she reached." She cried all afternoon that day.

She thought a lot about her father this weekend. She thought the reasons why, in the past and especially in the present, led him to isolate from the rest of his family and especially from her. The pain, the widowhood and maybe the lack of background to conduct the education of a woman's daughter, without the presence of his dead wife.

With her focus on the research, Patricia was distant in her youthful affairs when an unexpected noise was heard in the hallway near her door. A sound from some part of the human body seemed to have fallen to the ground. She'd put herself together and gazed with anger at the door. Exclusive anger, due the fear caused by that strange noise.

Moments later, she was at the door, avoiding turning the knob and trying to hear more than what was on the other side. She pressed her ear close to the door and began to probe a strange world to her. Vibration, muffled sounds and various noises seemed to fill all that wood depicting an invisible world that could be partially unraveled. She began to hear a small noise of breathing, a breath that became panting and more audible, as if there really was a person behind the door ready to attack her. The door groaned. Not just like a moan from the wood or the hinges, but an animal moan, half-human, something that could be considered alive, coming from an inert matter and molded from a cutting tree that was once alive. She shuddered and pushed the ear away from the door, though her hand remained on the doorknob. She clutched the piece of metal harder and turned it slowly, as if she was invading a house of another person, a strange and hostile territory. She could hear every spring of this mechanism reacting to its pressure, and the texture of that cold metal in her hand gave the impression of fragility in the face of a contrary force.

The door creaked open, but now it was more like a child's groan. She looked to the left which was the darker side of the hall that led into more rooms like hers and the laundry room. From there came a silence almost visible. It seemed that the corridor had no end and that darkness was eternal. She turned quickly to the right from which came a faint light. It was the way to the exit and to the rooms of Mr. Jaeger, the banker and Mr. Pacer. She just knew both were not in their rooms. She would not have anyone to claim to at that moment if she needed. She began a careful walk toward the light as concerned, as it was pointed out, "*What could have caused that sound?*"; "*Would it be a thief?*" She continued walking in fear and the hand scraped the corridor wall, giving her a shelter and a false sense of security.

When she reached the entrance room, where there was an old couch, she found a middle-aged man, obese and with black hair and deep dark circles under his eyes. From his little mustache she could see that his mouth was closed to words, but his eyes spoke about something. In fact, he didn't say anything, when she tried to talk to him something like a good morning greeting, after she caught her breath from fear. Her strange interlocutor was wearing a dark suit and emanated a strange odor, something between a lack of bath, flowers and vomit.

After she spoke, he slowly turned his head forward and stared at the opposite wall, seeing a picture that did not exist. Patricia looked at this invader and meant to be more emphatic:

- Good morning... Do you want something? She found strength to argue.

- Can I help you with something? She insisted. Thinking: "*How did he get into the boarding house?*"

Since there was no response, Patricia remembered her cellphone if she needed to call the police. She turned back to the corridor, always staring at the man who seemed not to care about her or to be interested... "*Is he deaf, or something?*"; "*What a strange man!*" She turned to the room and locked herself, putting the door between her and the strange invader.

Then, she jumped on the bed to pick up her cellphone. She checked the charge and the signal. If she heard that noise again, or if she was disturbed, she would have that "weapon" against the threat. But nothing happened next, for at least three minutes past.

She thought immediately of Rudolph. "*Where would he be?*", Even rare at this time, his presence calmed her down and gave some comfort. She remembered his smile and the following good things. Became more confident.

She decided to spy again, and now it would be ruder than before. Decidedly at once she opened the door and went into the entrance room but the couch was empty! Just a few small petals of daisies scattered on the seat where he had been. She put the hand there to see if he had stood up any longer, but the chair was as cold as her hand! No sign of that gentleman that was there before. She checked the front door and it was locked. "*Great! Security at last!* " She went back to the room again, as intrigued by this visit as she was surprised by her sudden courage. "*How can such a device change our state of mind?*"; "*Or would it be Rudolph's memory?*" She reached the door and stopped, holding the door knob. Suddenly she felt unbearably lost, something was looking at her from the darkest floor in the hall.

Something deadly alive and threatening! But how alive was she if she could not hear any breaths? She was still barefoot. And so she can clearly feel that she was stepping on something wet on the floor. She pressed the fingers toes down to the floor and made sure. When she looked down momentarily, she saw the wet figure of two footprints by her door, but footprints much larger than her five and half feet size. "*That's a man!*" Scared, she looked at the door that now insisted not open with her trembling and desperate hands. She looked to one side and the light never seemed farther away than it really was, and looked at the other, the source of her terror, and the darkness never seemed so close! From there, came a silence of the smell of meat that was stored in the kitchen. That her nostrils felt, making her mouth with a bitter taste. But even very silent and dark, she could clearly see the silhouette of the fat man looking at her down the hall. A shiver ran through her spine in a sense of imminent death.

The door opened and this time she screamed as she threw herself into the room´s security, trying to close and lock the door with her hands that did not obey the controls. She froze there for ten, fifteen... twenty minutes later, She didn´t know for sure. The phone in this fright running had been left out! *"My God! I have to get it back."* She closed her eyes with this decision that seemed to be the last one she would take in this life.

Put her ear close to the door again... Nothing! No kind of noise from the outside world. She opened a little gap in the doorway to peer into the empty hallway. It was not enough and that was why she was opening up more and more until she could see her cell phone lying on the wet footprints. Looking at this object, she slowly extended her hand until she touched it with her fingertips. Her little fingernails tried to drag the device closer to her. When it was finally in her hands she held it tightly and pulled it close to her chest. It was very valuable that time.

Before closing the door, however, she found that there were no other wet footprints to those footprints that were already at her door, either to the right or to the right. She shivered longing to hear the sound of the door latch closing, or a familiar voice on the phone.

On her mobile phone an SMS with an invitation to join the ATHOS network sent by Sinead.

12th Week

On that Friday, she thanked God, or upon the memory of faith in something greater she had someday. She thanked God for finishing another week, even though in the next week must have an ultimate test, with the presentation of her academic paper to a teacher's bank of the course. Not that she wasn't prepared, but the discomfort of presenting it and being sated by her classmates, was letting her up by a simple matter of maximum anxiety.

The previous week, she decided to tell Milena about her visions and current state of mind. How Milena had insisted on helping her, always asking, *"How are you?"* *"- Do you need help, don´t you?"*; *"Do you wanna sleep together?"*; It seemed now for such soft pieces of solidarity and brotherhood she would be willing to refuse no longer. The frailty and loneliness were making her more vulnerable to issues that pride and vanity tried to push away. She was always on by herself until she came across these unusual situations.

However, her participation in the Athos social network was increasingly consistent. In a few five days, she had fifty-four virtual friends, receiving daily postings, and at least talked to ten of them with a certain frequency. Charles, Sinead, Juliane, Robert and William were her favorites and those who could interact better with her. It seemed as if they knew her deeply for long time ago. The only issue that prevented them from interacting better was the fact that most of the contacts were only made at night. On weekends it was adequate, as long Patricia, for financial and academic reasons, avoided going out at night. But during the week, there were interactions that ran between classes or after classes when Patricia arrived at her place.

Patricia liked to stay, every day, for hours and hours, online with the new friends. With a lot of posts, photos, videos, tastings, and direct messages that looked like they were connected in a sphere of shared emotions. For Patricia, a real escape for their questions and frustrations. Never in her life had she met such fantastic people who filled the existence with truly interesting themes.

One of those postings caught her attention. So much so that she put it as a banner on her homepage of the Athos network.

"Worst to love someone alive is to love someone
who has already died!"

This phrase was read by her every night, and mentally, she always remembered her father, Rudolph, and her mother in some way.

In these nocturnal contacts during the week, she lost sense of the hours and lost herself face the force that came from the other side. She had just met new subjects, agreed with opinions, accepted facts. She would stay awake for hours, and often sleep after six or seven in the morning. She was so happy to have people, real people, to talk to at night, but she´s caught in time in a state of satisfaction, so the need to sleep just went out. But her body felt.

- Patricia, are you awake?

- Ohh ... Yes I am!
I meant to get some water.

- So you searched That link I sent you?

What? The last one?

- Yes! That one.
- What do you think?

- But these people,
did they really exist?

Of course Patricia, this is not
a theory, it's fact!

- Wow! How can they
do exist or survive?

-Paty, they simply
ignored the good, while

reactive behavior.
For them and their progeny,
only the death of their
enemies interested.

She was unbelievably thinner and paler! Anyone who knew her before, might not recognize her by now. Longer hair and face creased by furrows that presented the bones of her face. Her eyes had long since lost their natural glow, and her smile grew weirder. The hours of sleep were close to the beginning of a new day and noon. The lunch had turned into her breakfast. That's it! Only two meals in a day. In this way, she continued her lack of nutrients and low food intake, that's directed her to supplements and vitamins.

Milena arrived at her room right on time. Bringing a kind of folded document and some recommendations for Patricia to enjoy a small meal. Somehow she knew there would be nothing to eat at that place. The door had closed when Patricia got in her room with the result of a shopping at a bakery nearby. Stuffed biscuit, cheese breads, yogurt and iced tea. She stared and waited for Milena's approval for that fast arranged lunch. They sat around Patricia's laptop and her makeshift snack. The theme of that afternoon would be the calm and the need to present academic work.

Milena looked around at everything, and nothing caught her attention. Except a slight discomfort with the smell of the restroom and the general state of her friend. She had a pity for Patricia. Deep inside, she knew that she was not fully taking care of everything and she didn't have the mind structure to live alone and to study nursing away from her family. She clenched to that conclusion as the most viable for the case in question.

They sat on the bed face to face. Patricia took the initiative to start talking as she finished her second cookie, and having a juice to drink.

"Mi... I'm really doing no good! - Her eyes filled with tears.

- Patricia! - She bent to embrace her friend, comforting her by placing her head against his chest.

- Why didn't you let me help you?! - She whispered in a sweet voice.

- I'm desperate! - Patricia sobbed.

- Hushh! - Cry baby, cry that way we wash the soul.

- Nobody loves me, the teachers hate me, my classmates ignore me, my father gave up on me ... if I died ... nobody would miss me!

Milena at that point disengaged herself from the embrace and took her head in both hands, spoke in a solemn and amiable tone at the same time, staring into her friend's ejected eyes.

- Paty, please do not ever say such a thing! There are classmates who would miss you! Your father would die of longing, several family members like you! You can't even imagine how you affect them, either by your ability or by your beauty. You're special, you know? She paused for Patricia to lift her head. Don´t you ever speak of dying! At the end of her speech, she embraced her friend again, but now she shed bright, sincere tears of tenderness.

-And... I just can't take my life any longer! She burst into compulsive sobbing. - She leaned back in Milena's lap almost in a fetal position.

- Oh my dear, you might be strong now! - Patricia said slowly, cradling Patricia as a friend wept in her lap.

As much as Milena was struggling, her performance was the result of hours of continuous effort and maximum dedication to the studies. For Patricia, she seemed calmer, easier, with fewer hours of study, and more easily chilled to results superior to those verified by her other classmates. Even though, she is recognizing the limits of that person who was in front of her asking for comfort, care and affection.

Patricia could have a plenty of happy and fulfilled life, but there was something about that always compelled her to the bottom, to the dark and to an abyss of worries that undermined all her successes. Their merits lost their brilliance in a matter of seconds as they were transformed into pounds of guilt. Her mind seemed to work for her own ruin and disappointment. Nothing seemed to be helpful or perfect for her. What seemed to be superb or exaggerated pride for those who did not know it, for Milena they always sounded like problems of internal imbalance in that mental world that turned reality into something of extreme harshness.

Milena had only compassion for Patricia when she recognized her as fragile and helpless in that way. But nothing she thought of telling her seemed to make any sense to Patricia at that moment. This way, she felt that would be real in front of her, transmitting warmth and attention.

They stood in that position for several minutes, until Patricia's cell phone vibrated. As if by magic, she seemed to step out of a trance from the real world into another character far removed from her pain. She picked up the device quickly and resolutely, as if he knew what it was about. She opened the avatar on the Athos network and smiled briefly. Then she swiftly posted a response, ran her finger across the screen, three, four times, until he smiled again at something she saw illuminating her face, both in the physical sense and in the emotional sense.

After a few minutes, she turned off her cellphone and in time could recover from something deeper and darker. Finally she looked at Milena as if she had not been there all this time.

- What's that? - She asked curiously with her friend's gaze.

- What were you accessing? - Milena asked, intrigued by her friend's change of mind.

- Nothing. - Patricia felt overwhelmed by her friend's question and felt it was time to end the visit.

- Paty, you've been in complete despair and helplessness for quite a while and now, you're normal and you've smiled many times, what's really going on? - She asked, looking into her friend's eye.

- It's a new network of true friends that normal people do not have access to. Only selected and invited people. People with a distinct and critical profile like me. - She used speeches and phrases from the network to put together a catch phrase between her and Milena.

- What´s the name of this network? - Milena turned away from the critical point of the subject.

- Athos. - She answered, rising from the bed and heading toward the door.

- What network is that? I've never heard of it. - Milena rose, too, and turned to her friend with her backs against the door.

- Then, my dear, if you've never heard of it, it's because you're not a selected, discriminating, critical person. She'd rather said that in a defiant, noncommittal tone, but she said it by opening the door as if to indicate the exit. For Milena, there was only an old sensation of shivering, as she had not felt for a long time, running her arms and the back of the neck. Not only because she had been almost absconded from her friend's room after she had dedicated herself to a fraternal task. But much from her mental confusion of having heard from Patricia's mouth, a tone of voice that did not seem to be exactly hers. *"Who is this person now standing in front of me?"* She gathered up his things and hurried down the hall, sure to look for answers another time. For now, not even a farewell would fit both. She would not be sure that she was saying goodbye to her friend or anyone else.

She left convinced of a new problem ahead and began to mind her talk with Rudolph. *"Yes, he immediately needs to know what is happening now!"*

13th week

This week, Patricia missed two days of class. There were no problems with scheduling or solving other issues, but it was the preparation for the final exams. Some teachers simply relaxed with the complexity of the classes and left the students more free to look for study by themselves, either in the classroom or in the library , or at home, as in her case.

She spent these days only in a nightdress and slippers and between an hour of study and another, she sought interaction on the internet, mainly by the Athos network. But it was useless. During the morning it was rare for anyone to be active online just like her. The network was more active after evening and nightfall. And in those moments of interaction, she just cherishes or resubmits her most recent or even the older posts.

She began to like and think about some themes and personal styles of each network member. There were "the funniest", "the most profound" and "the prophetic", those who "taught moral lessons", still those who posted pictures of sad and quiet places. They had their own style.

There was no mention of religiosity or appreciation of divine things. Patricia began to appreciate the censure of posts of prayer chains, little angels, or pictures of saints, that occurred within the Athos network, which would suggest that most of the followers would be laymen. Nothing more scientific and coherent, she always thought.

In this way, their increasingly constant interactions followed a more sober and cold orientation over all things. Even the photos of the participants' avatars were serious and profound, when not so much they were displayed in black and white. It seemed a certain internal convention, which Patricia joined in two weeks of networking. Turn your color photo into black and white image to have a sense of belonging.

One of these nights, she was watching a video clip of the band Avenged Sevenfold: A Little Piece of Heaven; some contact had posted. She thought, "*A young woman like me, at least.*" She was a little alarmed at the average age group she found. The Athos network usually had people of varying ages, but with a very high concentration of mature people. She watched the same video twice. And while watching, she reinforced a thought of the uselessness of life.

She made her mind to return to studies, but just before another music video. This time Pink Floyd: Us and Them; in a deep and soothing melancholy for her. Posted by a middle-aged person who seemed strong and vigorous by the photo. She liked this state of mind, being in the dark, alone and thinking of nothingness.

The cell phone rang one, two, three... She answered with impatience of those who wake up at this time:

- Hello.

- Hello, is Patricia? - A familiar voice spoke from the other side.

- Who is speaking?

- Patricia is your neighbor Elizabeth! - A lady said in an excited voice.

- Yes?

- Your father Patricia! - Interrupting the emotion with a weeping voice.

- What about my father? - She spoke even more coldly.

- Your father is at the Patricia Hospital, we don´t know if he'll take any longer! - and collapsed into a compulsive cry on the other end of the line. After a brief silence and after Patricia criticized the neighbor's cry with a mental reprimand about *"Who was she to cry for my father like that!"* She took a little deeper breath then said.

- Sorry about him. I'll see what I can do here, but still. Thank you for calling. - She finished the phone call.

At this time, only who would be right now in Patricia's room could saw the cold, distant countenance with which she uttered these last sentences. In fact, it was hard not to notice that her voice was altered. More metallic, but serious. It simply seemed that she was not the one who talking. Somehow, even in the dim light of the room, it was noticeable that Patricia was more bloated. Or something like this. Her arms were a little bulkier than usual. Her legs seemed broader and stronger than the straight, slender forms of before. Her neck had grown thicker and his face had changed. Her arm that held the cellphone had different curves and creases at that time, as in a still imperfect clay mount of human molding. A mount of muscles and tissues larger, stronger, but a dysfunctional arm, able only to hold that device against her head. But this act of holding was represented by two hands, one subtly over the other, ten fingers trying to hold the same device in a tangle of flesh and superimposed image that gave the impression of an aberration to the hand of Patricia. Her legs were four and the feet were mixed with another body type, making her old form a filling of a new being that can be sought. Two large feet, which would be shoes for Patricia's feet, standing her on the cold floor in a pose of power and fragility at the same time. In her new face, Patricia's rare beauty was no longer seen, only outlines of wrinkles and bumps as if her face would be lost forever. Eyes with two colors, rough eyebrows and a hooked nose. This was no longer Patricia, but a rough mix between her and the impressions of the photo of her Athos network contact. But she was the one who was very annoyed by the intrusion and the freedom of a nosy neighbor, and from her annoyance came a strange stimulus to anger.

She was upset with the fights, with the abandonment of her father. She was reminding each day on his lap the father just exchanged for work in hundreds of rejection moments. She was outraged at her mother's death, and the father was the only one left to blame for letting her die. She was disgusted with something that could be God to her. That He had let her mother die, and father was now withdrawing her, and that he had principally given her this miserable life.

They lowered the phone from their ear and smiled with melancholy and sadness. They stared into the dark of the room and felt somehow happy about someone's death. Their smiles turned into laughter, broken and choked with improprieties, then ended in a laugh that both fell on their knees looking at the ceiling, as if challenging something superior to despise life and existence.

14th week

As she had not gone to her father's funeral, she thought twice to try not to miss at least his seventh-day Mass, which was ordered by that nosy neighbor.

Without the natural formalisms, I was wearing only jeans and a blouse with more colorful colors for the occasion, or for those who would like to outsource their melancholic state of mind, maybe true or not. Since Patricia was marked by the useless sense of it all and wanted to get rid of those memories as soon as possible, she was just as neat as if she were going to any social meeting.

Walking down the street, on the way between the bus station and the church, she noticed that the town houses had "aged." They were "older", with less cared for. There was more grass on the sidewalks and less cleaning. As much as she knew it was still two o'clock PM, she noticed that there was few light that day. "*A dark day*," was all she could think of, as to all the feelings that came to her. The past, her present and an uncertain and uninspiring future. The shadows that poles and trees projected to the ground were far more than a light-dark contrast. Those who were more attentive, could see that the shadows were stronger, causing an impression of voids filled with the complete absence of light.

In this way, she was assaulted by two distinct kinds of emotions. They were two opposing forces digging into their consciousness in an intense and disproportionate way. On one side was a group of feelings and values that she had come into contact with after a conversation with Milena that had occurred three days ago.

During that conversation, Milena, already a little bit distant from Patricia since the last incident, was inquiring about the friend's insensitive behavior over the death of her own father. Thoughts of gratitude, family bond, surname, and dedication were mixed with calls to her heir, financial support the father lent her, and the need to value life, honoring the extreme. If she could not be present, for reasons of testing season and the distance when the father died, veiled and buried. Let her, at least, go to this last tribute and visit him at the cemetery. From this suggestion, the only place caught the attention of Patricia. Always jumped that wall, always hid in those tombstones, always got peace and quiet, sitting there near those who were gone.

On the other hand, there were newly acquired concepts about death, or about life here in this world. They were fragmented and had strong thoughts about the end, the transience of life, the injustice of death, or the denial of paradise or eternal rest. Patricia was assailed by very negative impressions of her feelings toward the past, which discreetly assumed an exaggerated disbelief about her future.

All these themes were very well ventilated within her new social network. Athos, who, coincidentally, had members of atheism, of wrong Spiritism, non-practicing Catholics and people who believed just in this existence.

But in these intimate conversations, which were being caught in the way of the church, however good the words and memories that came to her mind would try to drive away or overshadow the denser thoughts of rancor and heartache. That was the state where she lost herself in an intimate revolt against her father. "*I did not ask to be born!*"

When she arrived at the church, the biggest of the hometown, was a group of people talking and they recognized and came to her with a worried, tearful air. A series of hugs from people from her childhood, who were now wrinkled and curved, wearing dark clothes and displaying Catholic symbols.

They gave her a little folder with the memory of him. A picture of him: younger, alive and happy *"as he managed to triumph over death."* She started a deep thought just looking at the face that had once been familiar to her.

She walked with people in the same direction they were going. But she didn't pay any attention to the stories and facts. Until they reached the central bank of the church that was empty, apparently reserved for the relatives of the two souls who made the passage that week. Her father and another local lady guessed it.

The church was full and they could see clearly who would be the lady's relatives and friends in greater numbers, and who would be relatives or friends of her father, in a lower number. The mass passed in the same way as others. Quiet and monotonous, until Patricia had been invited to speak the second reading at the pulpit. She didn't know that she would be called or warned of it. But they insisted so much that she agreed to get rid of that harassment.

She ascended the pulpit to begin the reading of Job 10 (1: 9) still in anger at the insistence of her father's acquaintances. When she positioned the text in front of, a strange sensation caused her a slight dizziness. She didn't know if it was the result of the tiresome journey, or if it was because of her traditional poor food. But it was true that she knew that feeling that was bothering her right that moment.

As she looked at the paper in front of, the letters mingled and shuffled, making the text unreadable. Even trying to fix her vision and straining her eyes, she could not make out any words. She stammered *"It's..."* for almost four times before she began to narrate the text loud and clear for all to hear! However with a certain peculiarity.

She did not read, just recited. She didn't remember it, nor didn't she know the content of it, only opened her mouth and modulated the sound of words in the exact order in which it was written. Her frightened eyes were ejected and they looked at everyone as if crying out for help, while her calm, communicative mouth was deciphering that information. She turned her head to one side so she would not look at the paper and it would not work, she turned away so someone could come up there and help her, but nothing.

> *I loathe my very life;*
> *therefore I will give free rein*
> *to my complaint -*
> *and speak out in the bitterness*
> *of my soul.*
> *I say to God: Do not declare me*
> *guilty,*
> *but tell me what charges you*
> *have against me.*
> *Does it please you to oppress*
> *me,*
> *to spurn the work of your*
> *hands,*
> *while you smile on the plans of*
> *the wicked?*
> *Do you have eyes of flesh?*
> *Do you see as a mortal sees?*
> *Are your days like those of a*
> *mortal -*
> *or your years like those of a*
> *strong man,*
> *that you must search out my*
> *faults -*
> *and probe after my sin though*
> *you know that I am not guilty*
> *and that no one can rescue me*
> *from your hand?*

Some people noticed the great ability of the daughter of William Chase in decorating the text in such a short time. Others were even alarmed at the great knowledge of the Bible that she possessed, to the point of speaking the selected passage by heart. Others only listened in silence, now ecstatic with the meaning of this passage, now bored with the delay of worship.

Finally came to the end of the selected section. But she did not stop talking. She changed the sequenced words of reading by some of her own opinion. It was as if she had taken advantage of that brief moment to open her heart and give her thoughts about her father's passing. But not! Those words were not yet entirely her own. Something was compelling her to stay there and talk, her voice growing more powerful and serious, almost threatening. She designed it by stating the need for repentance and the search for light. The church was filling up with more and more of the faithful who were now arriving, appearing behind pilasters. They shied away from the evidence and walked shyly forward. Slowly, they entered through the side doors and the central door, walking solemnly and serenely to their seats.

They didn't look at Patricia anymore, who was already in tears by that moment, revealing situations of hurt and rancor of the souls that passed between the two worlds. Some people got up and left. While others were still coming in. Although there were no more places to sit, the new listeners crowded around the side altars and into the central hallway.

The church seemed heated with so much warmth that it would probably be human in a multitude of beings who wanted to be there to hear those words. But the tone now was still of the strongest threat and swear of persecution to those who did not want to follow a path of justice! "- *People with blemishes in their past, people with stains on their hearts, people with hands dirty with blood, people with memory ashamed by crimes ...*", all were cited in the words of Patricia. While the priest tried to hold the altar stone, widows and beatified women cried their lives as the crowd fell on their knees. Some even threw themselves on the ground in groans and moans.

Patricia was already exhausted when at last a very big and fat lady arrived, dressed in a long black dress that passed by all that gave her way in a measure. This lady came in a serene and distant countenance, with her long white hair, received in a beautiful black veil, which left her with the air of a widowed bride. He walked in solemn steps toward the altar, until a man in a very black suit in the middle of the road offered his arm to continue the walk to the altar. This distinguished gentleman, as he approached, seemed more and more to her father. Yes! He was really her father! A little younger, healthier and oblivious to everything that was going on. Her father appeared to his youth and this was fading as he got close to the altar. He was aging step by step until the final step, he was bowing, losing his human appearance and getting a cadaverous and emaciated tone. He really was dying with each step, turning into an amorphous set of bones and furs... This apparition was enough to make Patricia faint and fall behind the pulpit.

Gradually, she was supported by her father's friends and neighbors and taken back to her original accent. Being embraced and reassured by everyone, concerned about their state of health. When she regained some of her conscience, she apologized and pardoned the hard words with everyone!

- You're welcome! The nosy neighbor came forward. "- You just couldn't even begin to talk and fall to the ground!"

Patricia didn´t believe that! So she pushed the circle of worried people a little. She realized that the church was almost empty. There were no other guests but the few who came because of her father. There was no crowd and no obese lady wearing a black dress. That was nothing but a powerful hallucination. *"But if it was a hallucination... Why was my throat irritated and dry?"*

15th week

The days had passed to Patricia without some sensation of hours, in the gloom of her place, she didn't realize exactly what time it was, or what part of the day it was. Sure she was awake wanting to sleep and that her cell phone would ring when it was time to get ready for college. *"I can't take that class anymore!"* She repeated mentally as she kept navigating the Athos network.

In this network, she could already be considered one of the most popular and her postings received hundreds of likes. In one of them, the one that most caught everyone's attention was about her recent experiences in hometown, more specifically, those which occurred inside the church. Not just "likes", but several virtual friends posted their comments about those facts. Some with knowledge, others, however, frightened and confused by this kind of information.

Milena and Patricia almost did not speak to each other, not because Milena had changed, she insisted on contacting the friend in need, instead. Even in the way she looked, the attention and the many prayers made. But Patricia insisted on ignoring this kind of help, much for now having grown up within her a bad feeling that Milena did not want her good. She was envious" a *"poor girl"* who mirrored her personality to be *"someone in life."* It would be a sort of *"vampire of energy"* who wanted to see her down and the power to excel in class and, who knows, with her stolen relationships. Those were easy conclusions which Patricia arrived, the times when she thought of Milena.

Every time Patricia began this mental discussion about Milena, imagining her likely headed for evil, for vices, and for sex. Everyone could see clearly in Milena's countenance some discontent, or even frustration. In her connection to Patricia, wherever she was, maybe near or still so far, she simply closed her eyes and lowered her head with discontent and disappointment. It was as if she were listening to these unfounded criticisms of her. As if she were standing behind Patricia's door, standing in the corridor listening to her "screaming" those words. Definitely an abyss would be emerging between them.

After Rudolph began to trust more in Milena, he approached another group of friends, he moved away from Patricia as well. He had even moved to another part of town, moving to a noble and less violent part of town.

Patricia felt so bad about this new distance between them. For her, Rudolph was becoming something special, which should have an intimate and pleasurable sense. She would like in essence the coexistence and approach had a connotation of affair. "*He was not a bastard like everyone else!*" Patricia was thinking of seeing him in the college's corridor, even though he had not shown any moment of sensual affection for her. It seemed just a little bit of affection and attention. It just would not be perceptible the disappointment she was, but words and conclusions about Rudolph, if really there were those "others" she imagined in her relationship intentions.

She was not a good example of a person with several social relationships, or even of an affectionate girl. The conclusions about Milena, that she would envy her or would like to mirror herself in love terms would sound so absurd. However, this torn apart from both, considered with contempt by the old friends, had caused the death of something even more inside her.

At the end of the morning, she found a new post on your Athos network. It seems they were predicting their mental confusion about affective relationships.

> "Worse than being rejected in life is to love a dead person!"

When Milena was not along with Patricia, close to her studies and tasks, she was thinking a lot about her friend. Something, or some force compelled her to try to help anyhow. When she was calmer and serene, there was always an inner voice inquiring about what she could do to rescue Patricia.

At one of these times, she took the initiative to talk with other students about what her friend's social life would be like.

Anything! Patricia didn't talk to anyone in her classroom for a long time. She asked about her activity on Facebook®, and got a clear answer that she would be inactive, for many months she had not posted anything there. "*A personal page is almost inactive*"... It seemed strange, because the friend was always on the cellphone navigating... "- *Ooh that's! The other network! - but what's really that name?*" She tried to remember the time when Patricia had told her about this new network she had entered, but the name, it would not be any more popular, I should remember.

Then she began an almost frenetic search with people who could help. But she only found reflexes of her intention in Giselle, who could perceive her concern and manifest a minimum of interest in the case of Patricia.

It was through her that she asked to start an internet search about possible social networks that could remind the real name and then, was able to probe her friend's activities. That would be a perfect plan, but the failure. Almost three days of trials and no concrete results from Giselle. She had researched in every way, putting the name of the friend, her possible nicknames, put her description, she searched: "social network"; "social networks"; "Social + networks". All possible imaginable variations and: nothing.

Almost close to giving up, Milena noticed that Giselle already wanted to leave the house heading for college. That was when she remembered the names of the "friends" of Patricia mentioned: Charles and Sinead. If Giselle could cross this information with her friend's, she could better locate this mysterious network that simply did not seem to exist. She was happy with herself and with the solution presented, but she should wait until she returned to the night to do the research. Giselle said good-bye to Milena and went for her bath.

At that very moment Patricia's cell phone rang! It was a high-pitched tune, but for her it was so smooth at that moment.

If she were in deep sleep, she would hardly wake up. She was lying down, trying to recover something from a losing sleep, rummaging in the bed in search of more comfort, when suddenly she jumped to her feet. It was late!

Still in silence and in wearing her traditional clothes, her belongings, she walked the distance between her room and the bus stop. Not for the day, or because of the schedule, but everything was very quiet at their traditional bus stop. She thought of hunger, she thought of herself, thought of other empty people, when she noticed that she was alone. It seemed strange, because at this very moment there were always some people waiting there like her. The street was very quiet and she could only hear the sound of the approaching bus. Very slowly the bus pulled up and opened the door like a breath.

Watching the driver, she noticed that he was a stranger to her. Through all those four months of classes, she already knew all the drivers of that shift, even that whole line. He looked at her from top to bottom and smiled with a perfect yellow smile. He was a man in disguise trying not to be fifty years old. Thin and had deep dark circles around his eyes. He spoke to her with the horse, feeble voice of a smoker:

- Take a seat, please. - Then sought ahead again.

She went through the roulette wheel and searched for seats in the few places there were free. She sat down beside a woman who was crying. She noticed that, only two blocks later. She cried softly and pressed the tears with a green, dirty scarf.

Two more corners and she continued to cry and the bus stopped at every bus stop, but no one gave the stop sign then left. They just came in. One, two... Or maybe none. They were occupying their proper places on the bus. Patricia used the remaining thirty minutes until she got to college to access the Athos network.

Hello Patricia, how is the trip?

Hi, who R u?

Your friend from the network... Samuel.

Yes, I know, but I never talked
with u Samuel!

There is always a first time for everything.

How do u know I am?
inside a bus?

Elementary my dear!

Hmmm ...

Yes, I seek to my friends!
Hehe

Where r u?

Closer than you think!

Ohh... stop that!

Yes. One day we all stopped.

Call me later?

Very later.

While tapping, she noticed that there was something different on that bus. "*Where would be the noise?*" Usually people are loud, they talk loudly to each other and they talk on the phone, sharing all their most intimate conversations. But that afternoon everyone was silent. Not complete silence, for if she paid attention, she could hear the woman's crying from the side and some other moans, now close, even distant, always choking with groans or unbearable coughing. "*And the noise of the motor roams?...* Why was it harder and harder to hear something?" She did like trying to clear the ears and taking some of the hair out of them to pay more attention to the inside bus noise and nothing. But contrary, she sharpened her perception of the speed of the heartbeat and her choked breathing.

Something would definitely be wrong. She reached for the window latch and forced it in vain. The window did not move. She stared at the now blurred glass and tried to recognize the way as if it was near her point to leave the bus. She only could see old houses, dry and twisted trees, dark and dimly lit streets... but no familiar houses or buildings. "*Where am I?!*"

She searched the faces of the people around her and some were asleep, some awake, but in a kind of trance, unable to interact with the interior of the bus or their passenger mates. Women counted their fleshy fingers, girls crying with their bloody bandages, gentlemen who tried to hide dark liquids in their mouths, old women who laughed at their own hands! A true circus of horrors paraded in front of Patricia with her pains and odors.

The bus was now speeding, turning abruptly into muddy streets. It abruptly stops, throwing everyone against everyone. Mixing those people who were panicking! Inert and decaying bodies were thrown against other beings who screamed in despair, but not in pain. They wanted to get out of there, they wanted peace and justice, they wanted to be forgiven!

Patricia fell on top of the woman who was crying, but now she was serene. Patricia looked at her for a moment in those dark, deep eyes and saw all the pain of a mother who had killed her drowned children in the bathtub. It had been more than eighty-nine years since this young mother of twenty-four was crying. When opening her mouth, Patricia can see pieces of red meat with few yellow teeth trying to say:

- You´re gonna die!..

With a stinking breath, Patricia pushed her hard so that she would roll back to her seat. Useless, for her hands, as she forced the cloth, the skin and the rotten flesh loose black pieces of muscle fibers and showing yellowish bones. The woman fell apart in many parts just when she hit the bus seat, leaving hair, clothes and bones mixed. Patricia threw up her lunch right there on the floor of the bus at the feet of an old woman who was trying to get her up quickly.

She did not resist, she could barely stand. She looked at all the curious faces who were interested in her case. Late in the afternoon it was so clear and Patricia, standing and helpless at the college bus stop, let the bus go on, dazed with her cell phone in the hands and still hundreds of feet from what she once called a reality.

16th week

Every day that week, when she woke up, Patricia asked herself, "*What am I going to do today?*" Not because she was on vacation, or having a day off, neither duties, she only despaired of being alive and having no concrete perspectives. There was no hope, no logical connection of activities and an agenda of a plentiful life. Only fragments of interest and disappointment accumulated day after day in a sense of fragility against the future.

Thus she woke up at the end of the morning and went back to sleep. One, two... three times. Until there was no more sleep inside her body. Finally, she got up late, about two o'clock PM that afternoon.

Meanwhile, no matter how hard Milena tried in her spare time, the research through Giselle and other personal searches was always in vain. She didn´t get accurate answers or addresses that could lead her to this Athos network. "*But how?*" Always be surprised by the mistakes and misinformation. Giselle always informed her that the search was for "*page not found*" screens.

But more recently, she has changed the strategy. Now she was trying to find out through groups of experts that Giselle searched in discussion rooms that mentioned alternative social networks or other closed dating sites. Any clue, even with some letter or indication about the possibility of Athos. Otherwise, they were also appealing to other countries. They have tried a lot of extensions beyond .com: es; uk; in; uy; air; ch; mx; fi; fr; np; rw... and nothing!

Their available time together for internet access was not enough, otherwise they could produce even more. In a busy week, always running, Giselle, much more than Patricia, was so focused over the studies and on obtaining an extra source of income. After all, life in a big city is filled with small desires and big dreams.

For Patricia, there was not much beyond the despair of recognizing herself sick. "*Yes! I'm sick. Much more than I thought about the fact*", she spoke to herself almost aloud and at least twice per hour. It was a mantra that cemented memories and sequences of images of fear, dread, and loneliness that she collected over the past five months.

She always started with a mental picture of the "apparitions," and before her heart flashed with a startle of panic, repeating the same emotion of that moment in the memory, she repeated to herself aloud, "*I'm sick!*" It was not too difficult to conclude the impact of this statement on Patricia's countenance. At the beginning of this week, she would shed tears when she realized that possibility. Already close to the end of this week, she smiled in the mirror with pride of her state. "*I'm sick!*" Her eyes were already translating much more than a comfortable success, to an immense personal fulfillment materialized.

In between an instant and other she tried to concentrate on the studies for the final exams, she thought of how she had reached that point? What was the mind tricking on her, to present such cognitive and sensory deficiencies? A mixture of wonder and guilt dominated her reflections on the present state of mind, always tempted to associate or justify her with external matters. From the genetic charge of a crazy aunt, to the behavior of teachers and classmates who ever "ridiculed" her, especially Milena, Giselle and Rudolph. All ungrateful.

About Rudolph, his convictions were becoming clearer now. He was a profiteer and adventurer who never wanted anything concrete with her. Always solicitous and smiling, but he wanted one more achievement, a trophy on his shelf full of "*Broken hearts and miscarriages*". His creativity and ability to distort Rudolph's departure were far beyond the concepts of rejection, or refusal of relationship was a small hatred that arose in direct proportion to the platonic image she harbored for Rudolph, so let him would be entirely responsible for everything the sentimental disaster that represented her unloving life.

"*He never wanted anything with me!*" She said this as she rubbed the red pen in the study book, scribbling to the point of tearing a couple's drawing hand in hand, having a heart in the background. It was a mental excuse she had for the moment when Rudolph's image appeared in her mind. Otherwise, she imagined him in the arms of Milene or Giselle, to complete her field of hatred. "*How they plotted so she could not have a relationship with him!*" Always talking, always plotting... she remembered perfectly every moment she saw them talking together. "*It was Milena who suggested that Rudolph leave me! That envious one wanted him for herself!*" "*They were the two who isolated themselves, so they could live their secret romance.*" She also remembered the times when Milena praised Rudolph in particular with her. Insinuating, phrases, ideas, or male gestures! "*All faking!*" "*They were already arranged and Milena tried to throw me over to him, knowing that I would reject in my shy way!*" Her hurt over two of them could be felt or even seen, when in contact with that countenance with wrinkles.

She was in the bed with a laptop opened illuminating her face in the room´s gloom which had not been cleaned up for weeks. While gnawing her nails that were not being used, clothes, food remains, papers and books could all be seen in the most perfect disorder. The time had come for her to walk around the room naked, because she had no more clean clothes to wear. When she went to the bathroom, she just didn't remember whether or not she had cleaned the flushing toilet. The smell exuded dirty and sloppiness.

Within her network, the opposite, she was an honest, participatory, sensitive, and zealous person. She presented the advances in class, her results, texts of renowned doctors and impressions about life and love, which were very much liked and shared by everyone in her network. And in the same way, she always enjoyed and shared texts and videos of her virtual friends. For real and ever, the only friends she had.

She did not notice, but she spent more hours hooked up to her network than properly feeding herself, having fun or taking care of herself. Simple tasks of her day to day life were postponed for hours of delight on the Athos network.

Patricia was surprised by the growth of the network. Now it had more than a thousand members, but unfortunately a large part was strange to her, until the contact and the interaction began and increased. There was no predilection for age or gender. She talked to everyone with no distinction, but only with some of them she maintained closer and more fruitful contact. Many there, just asked things, facts or dates. They seemed inexperienced about the internet. To this strange world they entered.

She was scared in the middle of the night with some posts by newbies in her network: just screams! From one up to four minutes of shouts of the most varied types and timbres. When this horror session began, she moved around and searched for the older friends.

Charles was the most present, but Patricia never took an interest in meeting him personally. His photos showed him in the past and in the recent past performing projects, people and work of high complexity. There was nothing about his family and when she asked him something about it, he just "disappeared" for whole days. Until Charles have shyly come back, but still with this taboo about his family. She decided not to ask for more. Their subjects revolved around the anatomy, the diseases of the body, and the falsity of the real world.

Already with Sinead, who was more sensitive, the subjects were lighter, but not superficial. They talked about values, about inheritances, about eternal friendships and about family. She did show two children in her photo section and curiously she was now far from them and missing them. Since they lived now in another place, no longer with her, this was enough to awaken her ambitions to be a mother and to be able to embrace them well. In these posts, both ended up crying their impressions on the pain of loneliness. Sinead about her children and Patricia, somehow, about her mother she did not even know.

One of those lonely nights, Patricia did not openly ask Sinead to become her false mother. There was an eternity of silence in the conversation between them, but near the end of the dawn Sinead said "yes" in a post sent. They would be more connected since then. Patricia believed that Sinead would play the role of mother and Sinead focused onto her all affections as a daughter to take care of.

Sinead anticipated for her that she should believe in something superior that commands our lives and intentions, as well as worry about something more present and inferior that will always be in charge of obstructing our evolution, no matter what it costs. They talked about religion and Sinead simply regretted not having developed her faith enough to help her at this singular stage of life. She insisted that Patricia develop any kind of religion and meditate during the day.

Sinead claimed in the posts a vision of a black angel who always pursued her and tried to surround her on the street or in dreams. She laughed at his paranoia, but was concerned about how often and how intensely it had been. "*Am I crazy?*" asked Patricia in their conversation. Patricia, doing her part, felt comfortable and confident to describe what had been happening to her: the visions and hallucinations with more details and colors to Sinead to be impressed. And that, if possible, she thought Sinead found her much more insane.

At the night, Patricia described what had happened at her father's funeral and the facts inside the church, Sinead again disappeared for a few days and did not return to the Athos network. Only after four days did she return to contact Patricia and no longer touched on this subject either.

Then she was scared! It was close to nine o'clock PM on another day! She would be greatly alarmed at this connection of many uninterrupted hours... But then she remembered that it was already Saturday. And so she would not be late for any class. "*So good*!" She thought, turning the computer down.

In the lower left corner was the watch and the date of that day. Patricia was not late that day because there would be no class. But it was not Saturday as she thought it was. It was already Sunday. Patricia spent almost thirty-three hours turning on the laptop connected to Athos.

17th Week

The final tests have begun, and Patricia was not ready yet. Even with her dedication to studies, the behavior and routine didn't take her beyond in terms of content skills. Just a short time ago, her vanity was directed to be always belittling the tests and dismissing the college as futile and useless. She simply didn't try so hard, or reached to the point of trust in her abilities and the minimum knowledge required for each content. In her mind there were always two recurring thoughts. "*Who needs to proof anything?*"; "*If I lose my exams, I'll close my course!*"

She met Milena in the hallway and only exchanged of glances. They were always cold and distant, as if Milena was one of her noisy classmates. But Milena's were more significant and mirrored the astonishment at her friend's condition. Milena just wanted to talk to Patricia for a long time, but she no longer opened her eyes. She was very impressed with her friend´s extreme thinness, the lack of personal care, and wearing the same outfit for days.

She noticed that Patricia already had dirty sticking plasters on her fingertips, where one day there were nails. Today only pieces gnawed at yet another manifestation of extreme anxiety and sloppiness.

In one of these casual encounters between them in main corridor, Milena stopped and said:

- Patricia, I'm really missing you! - She spoke with a clutch in her voice, while sincere tears rolled down her face.

It shocked Patricia very much that made her stop and look at Milena with the old affection between them. It seems that the sound of a sad song has stopped in the head of Patricia and she can feel someone else's feelings for a moment.

However, once this trance that had sustained her and which had been for days was broken, she turned her eyes in the orbits and lost its ground. She fainted in front of Milena who threw herself to try to contain it from a drop to the ground. As useless as necessary, her arms only followed that falling body.

But once on the ground and already in the arms of her friend, Milena told her about affection, shelter, comfort and concern. Things Patricia didn´t have in her life for a long time. She let herself float over those sweet, sweet words as she regained the senses. She felt a kind of heat that could be coming from the body of her friend, who, with her words, comforted her in a different way. It was the awakening of a heavy, dark sleep. But some flashes could be seen lying on the floor with hair scattered around the head to look at the ceiling.

She began to put herself together and sat at the floor with her legs crossed listening to a friend concerned for her condition, clothes and hair. Then she saw a figure at the end of the hall where they were. She knew what it was about, so she looked away with a heart beating fast, turning her sight immediately to Milena, that charm would not fall into pieces.

Milena began to enter into the subject of the new unknown network and her concerns with Athos, which Patricia listened carefully even though she was increasingly bothered by the subject. Milena had presented the questions to her friend who began to have changes in the heartbeat, elevated breathing rate and a cold sweat on her hands.

- Patricia look, I'm very worried about your virtual network of friends. I searched a lot on the internet these past few days, and no sign of such a social network Athos! A true mystery... - She paused to pick up some of her thoughts again and mind how she would continue this theme with her.

- I think it's a network of people who do not have a proper social life, because they hide. I do not see members, I do not see posts, I do not see comments on mailing lists. Simply this network does not exist on the internet! - She finished talking in despair.

Patricia, with a flash of indignation, thought that Milena's speech was strange, "*What do you mean?*"

- I've been on this network and accessing it for a long time! - She took some courage and began a brief speech.

- Look Milena, I know I'm going through a bad time in my life. It won't be so easy for me... She was recovering her usual phlegm. - But do not worry too much about me, ok? I'm actually getting better. Thinking about new excuses:

- Since my father's death, I've been in the process of reviewing my life. My concepts and values. This is normal I guess. This time that we broke up our friendship, may be only a short pause until things get better.

Milena didn´t much believe in those words, especially when Patricia's tone of voice had changed from a feminine frailty to a rational, cold and distant argument. "*Like I'm talking to somebody else*". At this time, the hallway lights flashed, then went out for a couple of seconds.

When the light returned, Milena saw her friend standing, as before, no sign of animosity or appreciation for her. Patricia said coldly:

- Get up! - Staring at Milena.

- Who do you think you are to snoop around the personal lives of somebody else. People you do not even know! - Patricia had already raised her voice:

- We do not give you permission, by the way! – Oh! Poor girl. You can never enter our network, even if you want. Just insist on your pathetic need to help those who do not need it anymore.

Milena didn't understand Patricia's speech and her threats, for the simple fact that her voice had changed from a weak, feminine voice to a powerful hoarse voice. That seemed like ten people talking at the same time, so strong was the tune of those words. A cold shiver ran through her spine and lodged in the nape of her neck, which rose with fear. Who was the one in front of her? Or better… "*Who were those people?*"

Milena got up quickly and awkwardly and sought strength for any kind of confrontation without looking at Patricia. She turned to the opposite side of the hallway, leaving Patricia at some distance to stand and watch her.

She passed the entrance door feeling that it had come out of a pressure oven and passed now into warm, cool air. Looking back, she can clearly see Patricia was in the company of two more people. Or shadows of hazy figures that embraced her, holding tightly and confident.

Before she turned the head trying to look a way out, she felt a tightening of claws and teeth in her throat. Strong and sure made her bend to the knees, so she would not feel any more pain. She felt a putrid breath and a kind of ardor of burning, while an animal voice tried to imitate human speech: "*y-yyou mhust desah-pppierr*". Her eyes were becoming weird and turbid with the shocks she felt in the region of the trachea, but she could still see the three figures laughing at her and the situation.

She was already on the ground with both hands on her neck when she heard a whistle and this animal-being that attacked her stopped the hunt and turned back to her masters. With her face pressed to the ground and a kind of saliva thread dangling from her mouth, she saw Patricia and the strange dog-it, side by side, walking down the hall. She closed her eyes.

18th Week

Patricia watched the smoke from a bus being scattered through the air as she wanted to breathe out the air from the lungs. The memory of the exact feeling of being alive and able to walk upon those streets was enough for her that Tuesday afternoon.

Elsewhere in the city, Milena was now in pain, not only because of the strange signs of wounds in her neck, which should have been hidden from anyone who could see them, but also from the feeling of loss of her friend to something she could not describe yet.

Moved by a feeling of love and compassion, she sought in her prayers an extra-human force to help to pursue the quest, even though she was now a threat. Whenever she thought about that college night, she tried to associate Patricia with her weakness, lack of concentration, and affinity with Patricia to justify that subjugation in such a real and impressive way. *"Perhaps Patrícia's mental projection had been induced to me, that my sub consciousness had released an image of terror..."* However, her religious formation led her to a creation of a mental picture of diabolical possession that she immediately repelled, closing her eyes and thinking of God.

She remembered the years of instruction she received from her former teachers and other teachers of religious formation. They always touched on this subject on powerful work fronts devoted exclusively to evil itself. Her reaction, like other classmates, was one of concern, but without deep practical awareness. As much as they saw scenes and images, they didn't have the exact certainty of this power contrary to their good intention.

In this inner dilemma, which expressed an individual fraction of the struggle between good and evil, it stood as a loyal representative of good. She wanted to help her friend. Wanted to get further on this story. She wanted peace for herself.

She got on the bus the way to the college with Giselle who had just arrived. But she had not seen her friend immediately, because of a small crowd of people who had formed for the entrance into that transport machine. Only after being positioned at the bottom of the bus can you recognize the silhouette of the friend who approached you affectionately. She was leaving earlier this afternoon so she could do some research in the college's library. Milena joined her to give direction on the afflicted friend's case.

Inside the quiet, aseptic atmosphere of the library, she waited for Giselle. But in the meantime, she sat there recapping the research and the methods. Something indicated to her that she should ask Rudolf for help, but another inner voice indicated that she could handle this task alone. With a piece of paper and a strange pen she carried with her, she began the research again, but from the search for the dialogues. She set aside the information Giselle had confided in the bus. It was a new play, but it still could not fit into the themes of her new research.

Thirty minutes had passed, until Giselle leaned back in her chair. That's when Milena asked her about the e-mail she received that morning.

Giselle began to form her sentences indicating that a certain Robert, who claimed to be the victim of the Athos network, in his email, very extensive by the way for a first contact, said to have a relative who spoke about this network. In the beginning, she paid no attention to it at all, actually she thought it was of no interest. However, he asked more than twice that Giselle should believe in his words and did not think him as a crazy man. So he continued describing his cousin, after mentioning this network, assumed antisocial behavior. *"He was young and extroverted, but then he became introspective and moody".* Her aunt was complaining about the nephew's behavior, and especially his school performance. *"Gilbert simply changed from the daylight into the night shift..."* Milena, hearing those words, remembered Patricia immediately. *"He dressed in black and in the same old clothes..."* ; *"He let his hair and nails grow and he had not had a shower for weeks."* Giselle made a little face mask as she remembered certain parts of Robert's e-mail.

Milena, upon hearing this part, specifically thought that Robert was describing Patricia exactly. She listened to Giselle's interrupted narrative, which was beginning to show signs of weariness in remembering that content.

"He left school and his friendships and spent his last days locked in his room...", "...When he went out at night, he did not say where he went to go to and always came back wet or dirty with clay..." Milena instructed Giselle, who copied and pasted this email before continuing to read. *"...Once a day, he came home naked and all scratched, as if he were fighting!" ; " On that day, my aunt almost died seeing her son in that state! "; " She asked me for help and one day I followed him. I went to the entrance of a graveyard where he, without the least difficulty, opened the gate and entered. It was eleven-thirty PM..."* Milena frowned with a mixture of surprise and awe at the content that the email presented at that moment.

"...I was caught by surprise, the gate was now locked. I tried one, two, three times too hard to open it, but nothing. It was as if Gilbert had locked inside! I screamed his name, once and the second time... Two great dogs jumped out of nowhere together to the gate grille! They were black and big and I could feel their breath next to me as they barked. But what really scared me was the shape of their eyes! They were the eyes of a human being!"

At that moment Giselle stopped her reading to try to mentally imagine a dog with human eyes. She remembered cartoons, cute dogs, videos of dogs from the internet, coyotes, wolves, rottweilers... Suddenly, she was scared when she heard a dog barking in the middle of the afternoon, probably in the neighborhood hundreds many yards away.

"...I fled immediately to my house, trembling with fear on a hot summer night. When I got home I locked all the windows and doors, as if something was going to break into my house. I turned on all the lights and began to pray with my little Bible in my

hands!"- Milena tried to imagine the scene of a man in great fear, but the reading continued to invite her to read.

"*It was already three o'clock AM when the police called me on the phone. They've identified and told me if I knew my aunt and Gilbert. I answer yes, they were my relatives. They told me they were all dead, so the doorbell rang. There were other police officers taking me as a prisoner for their involvement in the death of my aunt and cousin!*" - Milena and Giselle put their hands on their mouths in concern for their safety of receiving an email from a person pursued by the police.

"*Today I respond in freedom to this process that was not the popular jury because I had preliminarily obtained a* habeas corpus, *based on the excellent relationship I had with my aunt and the evidence of Gilbert's imbalance. But they are still worried about the pictures that were taken at the scene of the crime, which showed the body of my headless aunt, sitting on the couch and a bloody frame resting on her neck. It was a picture of me and hers. Gilbert was at his side. Hanged with my aunt's guts!*" Giselle shuddered as she imagined the picture described in that email. She took a deep breath and the name "Gilbert" plus the words "youth" and "cemetery" and began searching on the internet. She did not know what she could find, but she was determined. So much in this case, because maybe almost two hours later, she found a page of a small newspaper reporting such a criminal case.

Yes! It should have been, but the names were not quite right... Richard was the young man who had been mysteriously murdered and Joffrey was an uncle suspected of committing that crime. "*He lied to me!*" She was very concerned that a dangerous suspect had her email.

The content of the report pointed to a mental disease crime, full of coincidences of dates and times. The investigations had not advanced much and the presumed accused would respond in freedom. "*Who could feel free of such an accusation?*" She thought.

She looked for photos of those involved. She did not find much of it, but a photo was taken of Joffrey´s testimony at the police station. He seemed to be a quiet gentleman, if not for the distant and cold look, she could even swear he was rather innocent. But she needed to see the boy, she needed to see the physiognomy of the imbalance.

Didn´t find it at first try, just the photo of the murdered aunt alive and smiling. Short hair and very obese. There were two pictures of her. A little younger with an air of happy and another older, already with a worn and sad face. "So... the smile is gone with time." Giselle told Milena very quietly.

But the boy, she knew he existed, but there was no footstep of him. She went looking for death records in their hometown. But she came to a restricted site that needed to be registered. She chose not to insist. She turned to open research again.

Ten minutes later, almost at the time of her last test, she found a picture of the boy. It was a not very recent photo, but it showed a completely bleak and sad person. Black suits, long, shaggy hair, untold beard, and deep dark circles. Very close to your uncle's description. But something caught her attention. It was the company that stood next to the boy. She was sure she had seen those people before, but just could not remember from where. Just clicked to close her landing page, when the start signal of your class sounded.

19th Week

Rudolph was at the door of the classroom, like everyone who was receiving the results of the papers they wrote. His friend Julian was as radiant as he was, since he had taken "A" in all topics, unless Patricia, who had six revisions for her paper, in all of the topics. So, one group was laughing and celebrating and she was furious at wriggling her clenched fists, believing there was some big mistake. Her anger could be felt yards away, although Rudolph had approached.

As she stared at her name and the results, Rudolph came over and, without her gazing, spoke softly:

- Did you know what happened to Milena? - He was looking at Patricia's face in outline.

- No. - She answered mechanically without turning.

- She was attacked! - He spoke intonation trying to make some of Patricia´s reaction.

After a few seconds, she finally turned to him and began to speak:

- Milena has always been a weak one, a desperate one who clung to an image of a victorious person, but who came from poverty. She is useless and suspicious. Do you think she would be immune to worries or accidents in this real world just for that?

She turned and walked away the corridor, leaving Rudolph stunned and perplexed. He tried to look to see if people had noticed that strange monologue in disguise. He was alone in that atmosphere of inhumanity, then he could repaired Giselle's name on that score sheet. "The biggest result in the classroom." "*...useless...*" - Patricia's voice came to her mind. He looked at the other results sheets and they´re always the same, Giselle among the top three best results. "*...useless!*" That seemed too much for him, to recognize the hatred stamped on her friend's thoughts.

That night, he decided to seek further information about Patricia and Milena, and why would they struggle? Maybe more details about the attack she had told him. He found out the thing got out of control since he's gone for a while. He thought things were under control and that Milena was doing very well. Deception, he blamed himself for not being able to instruct her, and still with excuses for not being nearer. There were no circumstances for blaming Milena in this situation, especially her inability to participate in what was really happening. Somehow, as a woman, she would have a better approach over

Patricia than himself. From that point he decided to change his strategy and intensify his vigil.

When he met her at the coffee bar, he apologized for the disappearance at the end of the semester and said he was worried about Patricia, especially after seeing her later that night.

- Milena, after I moved into a new form of work, I could no longer maintain direct contact with you, and especially with Patricia. I believe she is the one who needs our attention the most. - Speaking calmly and slowly.

- Yes! Did you see how bad she looks? - Milena leaned closer to him.

- Wow! We must help her, but she seems so proud of herself. I do not know how to do it. - He looked down.

- Listen, I've been researching some things that might help us with her. How about you and I meeting today to talk and to draw a new recovery plan for our friend? - She finished with a smile.

So they arranged to meet in Giselle's kitchen, which would be waiting for them, just after school hours. As she could get there earlier, Milena instructed Giselle to prepare.

Meanwhile, Patricia was still standing by the results sheet trying to reverse her results mentally. "*All wrong!*" She wailed, whispering, as she tossed her head back and forth discreetly in disagreement.

It wasn't easily repaired, but the shadows cast by her came from two different directions. Those provided by the side window and another, projected by the light coming from the ceiling. But there were three shadows that were seen! From this third one emanated signs and movements of hatred in gestures and grimaces, despair and revenge against them all. An inner, unrestrained voice that reached Patricia's ears unrestrainedly, made her tremble her hands as she imagined pictures of pain and mutilation for her enemies. "*Everyone!*" Involved in a bloodbath, they struggled in a dark, smoky room, which at that time already represented Patricia's heart.

Rudolph was now getting off the bus with Julian near the address Milena had indicated. Exactly at quarter to midnight, when his cellphone rang. Seeing Patricia's number, Julian decided to answer that call just to see what she wanted even later at night. He thought it was weird, but she hardly ever called him, even more at night.

- Hello Patricia? - No answers from the end of line.

- It's me Julian, you can speak Patricia! - A soft humming sound indicated that the line was still active, and that there was something on the other side. Even breathing.

He looked back and forth to cross the street that was deserted and went straight to the point:

- Patricia, I can still help you. In the name of old times. Just ask, or just let me act... I'm also worried about you! - He got safely across the street.

She stopped at the front of the building where Giselle lived and opened her backpack. In it was a bunch of keys with a red apple, which she had given him early in the afternoon. Even so, he decided to ring the doorbell so she would open the door for him.

Nothing! He rang several times. He finally accepted that she wasn't at home. He should come up anyway and wait for her watching TV. He opened the door and went up the stairs, which were dimly lit. He went to the second floor and searched for the apartment number two hundred and one. He tried to open the door, but the door was locked. He laughed at this attempt, for he would obviously be. He took the bunch of keys and began to try one by one the keys that were there.

On the way out of college, Giselle and Milena walked toward a bus stop, certain that they were a little late to arrive Julian and Rudolph at the flat. "*Wow, he's going to see that mess!*" Laughed Giselle, watched by Milena.

Sat at the bus stop, Giselle suddenly felt something bumping into her leg soothingly. She was frightened, and when he looked down she saw nothing. "*It would be a mouse!*" She was still searching for what might have been, when she heard a puppy barking. She can't identify where that bark might had come from, but it was a real puppy! A few more looks, and got up to improve her view of that place. Once more on her backs, she felt the same bump on the edge of her pants again. This time, looking down, she saw a beautiful Dalmatian puppy with a mischievous look on her. As she stared at it, it began to wag a tiny little tail.

When she wanted to bend down to pick it up, it turned away and went toward the street. Concerned, Giselle ran for the fugitive in the hope of finding her master. At the same time he looked at the keys, listening to a distinct impression from Giselle calling from inside the flat. A voice that at the same time pleaded, whispered his name. "*Julian...!*" That made him rush his search and at the same time shivering. "*Damn key!*" There were so many and each one looked exactly like the other.

The light in the corridor did not go out in its entirety, only diminishing its luminosity to the point of twilight. His hands were now trembling in a silent despair that seemed like an eternity. He looked away, looking as if he saw a figure watching him at one of the four doors of that little hall. "*Will you be a neighbor?*" He turned his eyes to the bunch of keys, only four keys out for that lock.

On the walls of the corridor, with the effect of the low luminosity, were more visible spots and scratches that looked more like a mosaic of distorted images. Faces, body parts, animals, teeth, and parched trees seemed to leap out of the wall for anyone to stare at.

He slipped the last key into the lock and it turned! "*It had to be the last! Damn!*" He made an entrance into the flat occupied by Giselle, certain to be being watched by a stranger in the hallway. His desperation, there was no stranger in the hallway, It was right behind him! He could see its silhouette as he slammed quickly the door behind him, trying to lock the door again. One, two rounds in the lock. It seemed that now he would be safe. "*Thank God!*" It was strange, not only to have thought those words, but also spoken them softly. Like him, an agent of science.

He looked for a switch wherever it might be. He turned it on twice, but no lights came on. Instinctively he took out the cellphone and made its screen illuminate the place. All almost normal. Cardboard boxes, stacked clothes, a dark coat on the back of a chair. Boxed books... He was speaking up to himself about everything he saw, trying to give life to that scene of loneliness. It all had Giselle as the owner, so cheerful and confident, and that night it seemed like a lot of inert, cold stuff.

He was taking the remote control of the TV and a place to sit. But he was at least comforted by the image of Giselle in his mind. It was a way for him to remind the friend who had studied with him in those last weeks of exams.

As he fumbled for a comfortable spot, Rudolph entered the room after a few minutes outside. He looked tired and worried about something. He watched his friend and waited for the best moment to try to communicate with him. When Julian concentrated on a spot of light in the room in the darkness, Rudolph said to him:

- We must wait, but you must be careful with your thoughts, if you lose control, our coming here will not make sense at all. He hopes for the comprehension of his friend.

- Yes, but please help me! – Said Julian almost in despair.

After a few moments he spoke to Julian.

- Of course! We are together.

Julian didn't notice, but his battery was almost running out and in close two or three minutes he would be out of energy for his cellphone's light. Things got worse, his cellphone rang. It was his current girlfriend who was worried about his delay and started talking about his day and his missing. Julian had no choice but to ask her to call him later when at home because his battery was almost over.

He no longer used the light on his cellphone to move around or walk around the room, blindly, groping and walking slowly. Only when it was necessary did he turn on the light on his screen to make sure what he was doing. He groped in every possible corner where a remote control would be. Meanwhile, Rudolph had a book in his hands and he tried to remember themes and texts about calm and relaxation. Her presence there initially would be more connected to Giselle and Milena than to Julian, but from the entrance he felt there was a sense of insecurity and a veiled threat to that task. Something could be very wrong that night. Something deadly wrong.

Julian tried to distract himself, found nothing but a red-captioned notebook. In it, in the faint light of his cellphone, he found Giselle's notes about her impressions of Patricia and her pursuit of the Athos network. He could not have noticed, but as he read such notes, there were two other faces behind his head reading as well. Illuminated partially by the brightness of his device. They pointed and laughed at Giselle's texts. In one of those chuckles, Rudolph and Julian became aware of what's in that flat too, but nothing was seen for a moment. Just that the chair was now without the dark coat on its back. Julian stared at the empty chair for a few moments, then turned the light on his cellphone to a hook behind the door. The black coat was there.

When he reached a few torn pages, he noticed they were filled with little drawings of Giselle. Drawings a woman would made, cute and delicate drawings. Nothing more written, except internet addresses and links. Page, after page, came to more obscure designs. Drawings of mouths, bones, phalluses and knives. Scribbled drawings, confusing drawings, and drawings of menacing eyes. He saw in a corner of the page a name of a person and the word e-mail.

At this very moment, the light of your cell phone will decrease to the critical point. He could not light up a hand in front of him. And it was at that very moment that he heard a chortle in the room.

- Who's there? - He tried to contact shadows and boxes. - Show up! He spoke almost in a threatening tone, for which he was afraid.

He mentally called for Rudolph to see if he could answer it promptly, but it seems he was busy at the other end of the flat. He called aloud to demonstrate to himself and others that he would be accompanied in some way. But Rudolph didn't move!

He turned to the exit door as soon as he could and he did not find the dark coat hanging on it. He was frightened at the recent memory that the coat was supposed to be there. He fumbled for the bunch of keys to unlock the door and ran away. But this time he knew the right key. But the labor was to put it accurately in the lock. His hand trembled as he felt an ever stronger presence of something behind his body. He felt a cold breath and a small touch of cloth on his left shoulder. It was the dark coat, which floated right behind him, as if it were being worn by some spirit.

The key came easily into the lock, he smiled with satisfaction, not wanting to look back! But as she turned the key, it broke inside the lock. "*Damn!*" - In desperation and anger he felt the sleeves of his cloak wrap around his belly, beginning to tighten his navel. He turned and was assailed by a hideous sight of a dark being, no eyes or mouth, no ears, or nose, which appeared threatening only in his intention to look as a human. Two deformed hands appeared at the ends of the sleeves and held him with superior strength. He rose from the floor close to the door held by the being of the dark coat. So he did not understand, when she saw Patricia clearly lying on the bed, dressed in a black dress and looking away at the ceiling of the room, laughing at all that. He was loose in the air, a drop of inches and minutes of memories of life. In discomfort of lack of gravity and pain of death.

The coat fell to the floor, but his feet immediately did not. They debated at the door three times quickly. He had the nape on the hook of the door for a few moments before he dropped dead from where that black coat was.

20Th Week

The test week was normal and without any kind of additional theme or subject that couldn't take everyone out of tune in this latest scholarly effort. In fact, it could be seen in the semblance of the students a desperate weariness offered for better results and hopes in the future.

Everything seemed fine except for the general nuisance of Julian's death. His usual chair lay empty and filled with flowers, notes, papers with tickets, necklaces, bracelets, and pictures of the students who wanted to pay homage to life, even if they kept this certainty of death.

Giselle got a medical license and was doing her exams at the course office, away from everyone and the memory of her friend. Even though she was too sad to stop for a few moments to wipe away the tears that clouded her vision.

Patricia performed the tests in the same way that she led her life: as if there was no one else in the world, except herself. She sat in her chair, which was purposely pushed aside by her classmates, due to her traditional bad smell, and the inability to cheat in the exams. In fact, they discovered in time that she had the ability to pass wrong results for the others, even for some kind of lack of skills or maybe simply evilness.

Patricia didn't even look at Julian's empty chair. She was no longer bothered by this absence after his death six days ago. What disturbed her was Giselle's absence at her traditional place. She tried to look for her during the tests many times. *"Where did that little traitress´ gone?! When I need her most!"*. But she's not the only one absent that moment. In her mental confusion, nor Milena's pleas were enough to get her to concentrate on the evidence and stop pursuing Giselle mentally.

Just leaving her test last Thursday, Patricia went straight home to seek refuge on her social network. She didn't want to review the contents of the test, or search for answers on the internet, trying to contact anyone about the tests either. She just wanted to make sure there were friends to have fun that night.

Otherwise, the network was preparing for her logon, since a few hours ago, when the first contact with her was made that night.

In these contacts, Patricia needed to listen to ringing or cell phone messages to no longer occur. Simply, Patricia could see that there was someone, or something, just trying to communicate with her inside the network. In her intuition, she was called to search as quickly as possible for an access or to enter with her cellphone to receive affection, attention or instructions on her conduct aligned to the network plans.

At the end of that night, it was no different. She was traveling inside the bus listening to Metallica's Fade to Black, already imagining the people who would be with her soon. It seemed to be a kind of trance with high expectations, one of the kind which we have when one's great expectations is very close.

Patricia changed her state of mind by focusing on the conversations she was having. Especially with Sinead who was indicating to her that she was being watched and that soon she would receive a kind of promotion.

Yes! Patricia, this is a
kind of goal of many
like you!

But how it come this promotion?
Simply girl.
From a moment,
you can order and ask to be obeyed.
You do not have to take orders anymore.

Who will give me this promotion?

Your behavior is the key.

No! There are qualities in you that
you didn´t realize.

Oh really! Trust me just
few more days!

Do not worry... She'll come!

Patricia got off the bus near her address, with a strong anxiety for the night of "promotion" could be that one.

When she got home, she threw the things away and went barefoot inside the room. She threw herself on her bed and turned on her laptop.

Ready! It was now connected. No hunger, no cleanliness, no prospects, but attentiveness. *"Tonight would be something special for me".* She felt so!

She saw all the messages left by members of her network. She accepted four more virtual friends. She responded to three more direct conversations and posted two photos of her expectations for tonight. One of them was very festive, but portrayed the Day of the Dead in Mexico, a carnival of celebration to life. And the other stamped some Inca mummies with the words: " *That´s for such a long life!"*

When it was three o'clock AM, something different was starting to happen. Patricia, who was always awake all through the dawn, began to yawn and to enter an unprecedented state of torpor. First it was a tingling of the feet and cramp in the calves. She started to have some abdominal pains, very much like cramps and since then she started to sweat cold. Her hands were even colder, then she lost herself and the feel of motor control of her limbs. Until finally she lost the sense of reality and ground. The room began to float and the walls changed in shape and color. She was delirious in this new distorted reality, where there was no matter, no body. Everything was mixed in past, present and fear.

After a risk of blood began to flow down her left nostril, Patricia, already sweaty with her wet hair, tried to get up from the bed, but immediately fell to the floor, cutting off her right eyebrow. Blood sprouted in filets that blocked her view. But it was enough to see an alligator crawling through her room from the bathroom.

She was not afraid, just tried to scream to scare it off. Her voice was kept to herself in a hoarse groan as it was getting closer.

When it got near her face, it opened its mouth and showed dozens of yellowish reasons for her to fear that moment. They were pointed teeth, framed in symmetrical rows, ready for use. But, however, they only let their carnivorous breath fill Patricia's lungs.

She didn't know how long she stood there to see that animal and part of her throat. But it was enough to establish mental contact with the creature. It was a different conversation, in which this strange being seemed to show appreciation and affinity with its present prey. It seemed, even in a menacing tune, to ask her to calm down and breathe slowly. It demanded she try to see it as a good friend and admirer. That it was there to purify her in a little necessary procedure for her next condition.

Patricia couldn't do so much. Her physical condition resembled an epileptic crisis with overdose tones. Breathing quickly through her mouth, the concentration was only in line with survival and the wish that everything would be resolved as soon as possible! "*Bite!*" It was what she just could think as the tears streamed down her face.

Suddenly, the alligator was erect. It was in a bipedal position with its lower limbs more developed and strong. It had arms that resembled a human being, and its features became a mixture of reptilian and humanoid. Its words were now perceived and heard by Patricia, but her tone was guttural.

He-it took Patricia in his arms and laid her on her bed. Then he-it undressed her slowly, until she released the dirty clothes. At that moment, Patricia passed out and fell into a deep sleep with her vital signs far below a waking state.

She didn't know what dreamed about, or how long her sleeping lasted. She just knew waking up on a beautiful sunny morning. Her face bathed in the sun. She was happy, nourished, free of her clothes and other social conventions. There was a certainty in the air that there was so much more than a simple life to live. She was plenty happy... *Was that the promotion ritual?*

When she felt the morning wind, she finally remembered her room and the night she arrived from college. She brought her hand to her face, looking for cuts or body parts in pain. But nothing! There was nothing on her eyebrow, nose or arms.

She was frightened by what she saw when she stood up. It was an open field with trees and horses grazing in the distance. She was stronger, confused, and naked very far from her home.

21^Th Week

Patricia had finished her last test the week before, and she was in some atmosphere of certainty that had made good tests. A sensation with a subtle blend of pride and power emanated from her, from the absolute best results of the class. She would finally prove to everyone that she was still an excellent student, despite her little more than forty-six pounds.

While the final results were not displayed, she was lost in the hours of contact with her virtual friends of the Athos network. She barely left the room, either to buy food or to pay bills either. Underneath her door, even letters and more letters of judicial notices about her inheritance and overdue bills were accumulating. The only thing that was quitted was her rent.

Her neighbors, from time to time, knocked at her door to complain of the stench she always exuded the night of that room. They wanted to know if she was alive, or whatsoever. They knocked at the door with more anger, than proper respect or some human interest. With their handkerchiefs or hands protecting the nose, their disfigured eyes of hatred for Patricia and her foul-smelling presence, were not enough to pull her out of the trance. She never did not open that door! Every time she closed the eyes to isolate herself from the outside world. Despite this, from time to time it is refreshed by the neighbors. Or sometimes she screamed at everyone to leave and leave her alone. Or sometimes, there was no one at the door in the midst of those attacks against her. Things mingled between the hours, the reactions and the two worlds.

On that particular day, everything was very quiet. Until that time, no neighbor or visitor had expressed any opposition to her smell's room. She was concentrated in her network, but looked every minute at the door. Not that she expected anyone to knock, but the silence of that door was bothering her. A silence within a smell of smoked and meats that are no longer alive. She was expanding her awareness beyond those walls, but going against something very morbid.

Giselle, despite her classmates, didn't complain about the outside world. She had barely shut herself down for the things of the earth when she knew of the death of her friend Julian in her own place. She was perplexed and lost, something between the pain of loss and the memories. She was sleeping with analgesics because of that bad news. So much, her routine was going to her internship then going to the police station to testify. There were only a few hours of resting provided by the remedies instead. She was up to the limit, but much closer to discovering something about the mysterious Athos network.

In these moments of human weakness, she found help in Milena that came in contact with her and tried to calm her, with words and affection.

Since the evidence was over, Giselle at least may have more free time to further intensify her research on this network. It was that kept her still alert and away from the impressions of death left in her room. Lights on, sound on, flowers... She tried to vivify that this place last week was the scene of a fatality. She would stay home most part of the day by sifting through websites, people, and facts that could help her. She even ran ads on relationship sites, discussion forums, and blogs so others could help.

In her computer, a photo of Julian can be shown, and a file dedicated exclusively for the network Athos are displayed at her top desk. She had a hundred files and photographs as well.

She couldn't draw a precise conclusion yet, but she was quite sure that joining the Athos network was related to a small coincidence of mysterious crimes and deaths during the last five years.

Elsewhere in the city, Patricia was online on the Athos network receiving comments and tips from her friends. One of them posted:

If you wanted an enemy of yours to be removed from your path, what would you do?...

She clicked on the person and started a chat:

-Hello! Who r u?
- I'm a friend of you on this side.
- Ohh... who do u know?
- Almost everybody here!
You must have heard about me.
No I don't think so... Julius?

-Yes, Julius, at your disposal.

Is that serious? My enemies?

I've never been so serious all
my existence!

Oh, I just wanted to scare who
thinks I'm crazy.

- Yes! A fright of death! LOL

- LOL, yeah! So they never snooping
my life!

- Your wish is my command!

Then he hung up, going offline.

Patricia found that dialogue quite strange. *"But what is not strange about this network?"* She laughed.

Giselle, at Milena's request, had just sent an email to Patricia with a list of dead and murdered people she had encountered, when suddenly she heard a crash at her own door! Exactly by completing the click on the "enter" key, her door seemed to be spanked! She gave a little jump out the chair, and in a state of shock she screamed scary. She got up from her chair and walked slowly to the door. She heard nothing more than her breathing and the pulse through her temples. It seemed an eternity until she reached the door. She looked through the spy eye and nothing. An illuminated corridor seemed quiet.

Turning back to her chair, she heard clearly a small dog whine and sniffing under her door. She stopped immediately, a shiver running down her arms. *"Where is my cellphone? ... I need it now!"* - She went towards her device, then she heard nails scraping at her door frantically as if a dog was digging a hole, that sound lasted until a loud, loud barking can be heard.

So she just reached out her cell phone and tried to start it up. But it was in vain! It was out of charge. The whimpering returned in supplication to be able to enter through that door again. She went back to the door, foot by foot. A deadly fear installed within her. She did not want to believe that for real, some supernatural or surreal thing was happening.

She reached the spy eye and forced her sight to try to see things out of her imagination. There was nothing again in the lighted corridor. Then she decided to open her door up, but before she took on her college things and sought a scalpel as her weapon of defense.

She was armed now. She was convinced that she could defend herself against everything. She opened the door very carefully, so smooth, making any noise. When the light can pass through a gap, she saw a shadow passing from side to side. She forced the door back as an immediate reaction to her fear. She looked again through the spy eye of the door and saw now a corridor in the shadows and a gentleman standing very close to her door! She screamed with dread, moving away from the locked door. But in vain. Two, three steps back with her scalpel in hand, bumped into a being that was inside her room, dark, bigger and stronger than she. It looked like a Rottweiler erect and two feet high and had the odor characteristic of a dog, but at the same time with human forms. At that moment she saw a horrible dog-creature leapt over her and grabbed her throat to choke her.

She didn't know how long that action lasted, but she felt even comfort when the pain has gone, and a small, faint ardor came up. It was so sweet, liquid, and hot to taste. A taste of blood could be proved and sipped, until she cannot breathe anymore. The mind calms down, it screams without sound and goes away, forever numb and asleep.

Two days later she was being sewn by a medical examiner who was wailing how a young woman with a promising future in nursing could withdraw her own life with a scalpel cutting her throat. She shook her head as she removed the gloves, threw them into the wastebasket in a mechanical gesture.

22th Week

From her laptop upon her bed the song Only Happy When it Rains by Garbage sounded as she was waking from the squatting position she was in, peeing in her bathroom directly into the main drain. Her toilet was so dirty and clogged that she had been using it for days.

The song paused along with a video she received from a newly-acquired friend on her Athos network. And it was still thirty past five o´clock AM, the net was very active.

In this video, in a tone of macabre irony, videos of the holocaust of the Second Great War were interspersed with newer videos of animal slaughterhouses. With scenes purposely edited to be similar to each other, the melancholic music I'm not in love by 10CC, twisted the horrendous scenes into a sad irony. Patricia smiled as she still listened for the third time and marked "like", as well as sending it back to the rest of her network.

So the night dragged on. She no longer had taste or virtues worthy of being articulated while she was awake. She had developed disbelief in almost everything except the opinions and suggestions of her virtual friends. Those, before the end of the dawn, sent a direct message. With the following question:

- Why not do you ever give up to
that stupid little college?

When she hung up the laptop to lie down at about ten-thirty o'clock AM, she saw that question written on the ceiling of her room until she slept prostrate for another full night of insomnia connected to the internet.

Well it didn´t mean to say she immediately fell asleep at the new day. It would be to try to shorten two hours of disturbances and sharp thoughts that kept her still aware and bound to this world. She actually went to sleep deeply at almost noon, entering a dream with all the characteristics of a good nightmare. All her virtual friends seemed to surround her in some kind of court, some vehemently attacking her, others just watching. Only three of those were defending her. Sinead, Charles and now Giselle, who mysteriously appeared in her dream. It had never happened before. When she "heard" her voice before the court, she thought to herself, "*but wouldn't be dead, would she?*"

She is quite not sure, the end of that bad dream. They were becoming very common for weeks now, but she woke up in the middle of the afternoon with the impression of having dreamed of dead people. People who once liked her and now they were dead. "*...My mother!*" She should have dreamed of her mother. As a tear rolled down her face, she was convinced that she should have dreamed of her mother who was defending her from danger and criminals.

Then she thought of her father, who, despite the coldness of her last years, liked her. "*Would be in my dream too, wouldn't he?*" She thought about his death, and the moments when she had been deprived of his presence. "*If he was alive... I could return to that house.*"

Then she thought of Giselle and Milena. Strangely and unusually, as she remembered the faces of the friends, she spelled their names very softly. You just got that picture in your mind. Her memories of the walk they both had made that semester were summed up to a fixed glance from Giselle in her mind. "*Dead!?*" she repeated to herself in a low voice. "*She shouldn't even live on in my memories.*" But Giselle did not leave. It remained "engraved" in her mind throughout that whole day.

She already resolved to leave and go to college that night to give up her course. Patricia tried to imagine whether she would be hungry. Even if she was, the odors coming from her room would not help anyone develop appetite. She dressed up and went out the door, stepping on her mail at the door.

Once Inside the bus, she tried to be sure nothing strange would happen again. She kept looking at those sad, distant faces, projecting defeats, frustrations, and justifications for so much gathered helplessness. For those who spoke, she imagined the densest defects of character. She talked to herself, but soon after she talked to the person next to her. Normally she received a glance of non-sense, but after a few more blocks, the person right there could answer and agree with her subjects.

When she got off the bus, people turned their faces to the window to keep an eye on Patricia. Among other thoughts of compassion, they imagined: "*It is sad to see a young woman so disturbed!* " ; "*God set me free to be like this!*"

From the empty chair where she was, only a shadow smiled at having fulfilled her mission of accompanying and keeping her persecuted in focus with her decision to drop the course. A couple sat on the empty bench left by Patricia with her characteristic scent.

At the college office she applied her quitting documents in a quivering, quick handwriting. She did not want to be seen there by anyone. Although there were people around her, she made sure no one there was familiar or even from her own class.

She signed the papers and got up to feed them back to the secretary on the desk. As it was at the end of the semester, she won't be able to answer any questions about that decision. Much better to her! She didn't want to give reasons why to anyone.

But just outside the office, she came across a roommate. She didn't even know her name, and just tried to be social in her conversation. This was partially resolved by her interlocutor who insisted on pulling a subject. Soon after Patricia's third step toward the door, she said to her:

- Did you know about Giselle, didn't you? - Telling as if was the most important subject in the world.

- No... What happened? - Patricia has shown some attention for a few seconds.

- She died! - Her classmate told her, trying to recognize emotion in Patricia's reactions.

For an infinite number of seconds, Patricia stared at her colleague's brown eyes as if he did not believe her words, or as if she hated every cell of that creature that spoke of his only friend in that college. The brief silence between the two was broken by Patricia's question.

- How did she die? - Her voice had changed to a tone of false curiosity.

- She was found dead at her apartment. Look, such an irony of fate, to rent a place only yours, and soon later... It seems that place is haunted, a damn inside. She was lying on the floor with her throat torn and a huge pool of blood. They said the cause of death was the drowning of blood, but the areas affected by the hypovolemic shock of her brain would respond by breathing and by the reflex act. It's a hard, very instantaneous death, if that piercing object were more than four centimeters... I doubt she even had an accident. Seemed like a criminal, indeed. But what would she was doing alone there? Did she have anything to do with Julian's death? Is it very strange, isn't? Her colleague suddenly stopped her trance of communication when she realized Patricia was tearing.

That tear was not exactly related to the confirmation of the death of the friend she already knew in some way, or the fact that she had lost a friend. But from the strange feeling of being inside Giselle's apartment, from her entrance to her last breath. A perfect series of images came to mind when her classmate began the narrative. It was not quite exactly what she told her. Patricia saw perfectly how everything happened, detail by detail. In her visions the room was not dark, so little Giselle was alone. She saw her among six other "people" moving, sometimes hiding and sometimes attacking. Until the final outcome of the scalpel nail she committed herself, trying to kill an animal that strangled her. She heard the screams of

Giselle's pain and the sounds of her flesh being cut with force and despair, as blood gushed down her throat.

She saw the faces of everyone there laughing with satisfaction. Even the face of the dog-it who was panting with its open mouth dripping saliva and blood. She had seen that strange animal before. It was familiar and well-known. She just couldn´t remember when.

She didn't say anything more. Nor even say goodbye to your colleague. She left her talking alone and turned to the exit. While she heard a sad *"- See you later..."*; She thought quietly *"Farewell! Don't you know it was the last time I saw you?!"*

She went back to her house, because it was already night and she wanted to join her network to talk to her friends and tell them about her new achievement. Get rid of the nursing course and the falsehood of your classmates. Now her destiny was back to her hands. She thought.

23th Week

On that Wednesday, she decided to take a day off entirely for herself. Not that her other days didn´t have such intention, but especially that Wednesday would have the luxury of doing nothing more than what really interested her. So, she made a short list of desires and priorities that she thought were being postponed for so long ago.

The first task on her list was to clean up her bathroom. Steady and determined she gathered the rest of her strength and began the task of keeping that part of her place at least presentable to herself.

With gloves, bucket and cleaners began to set direction to her desire to take more care of herself. In the middle of the cleaning effort, she had the idea of turning on the shower to use hot water to improve her cleaning performance. But before, she decided to use her cellphone as a sound machine, and with headphones, she would listen to some music. Sad, but songs.

While playing the Killing Moon by Echo and the Bunnymen, the steam was already dominating this room, while she with a small brush wiped small corners of her floor completely distracted by the task and the music.

The new density of air surrounding her favored a new atmosphere of wrath, heat, and agitation so that her thoughts could simply create colors and shapes in that dense layer of moisture. "*Would it be a face?*" She was startled when she looked in the opposite direction and suddenly saw an almost human form staring at her. But the quicker her impression, the faster was the modification, disappearing the shape of human appearance, due to the waves and movements of the steam itself. She gathered herself together, laughing at the acceptance of the phenomenon.

With her backs close to the wall, she just can´t clearly perceive a series of mouths and teeth that appeared and disappeared in the steam curtain. They were small signs she wasn't as lonely as she may think.

When the vapors were already thicker, arms and hands were already randomly traversing the body of Patricia, not only with more sensual appeals, but rather passing through vital regions in order to steal her vitality. Hands came and went over her ribs, beneath her breasts. Arms were trying to strangle her, but then they would dissipate. Patricia didn't realize this strange movement of gasses and moisture around her, only felt comforted by the heat around her.

Turning the shower faucet off, and in a few moments all that remained was the silence of the damp room. She sat at the toilet and thought of her solitude. In its uselessness that settled, limiting every movement, every piece of dream that one day she had. She was "alone", and the only idea she could think of was to try to find another mate for Giselle's "vacancy" as her best friend in this physical world. It would be a new mood for her that intended to stay there for a few more months, before finally leaving and trying to find herself somewhere else. She was torn between accepting the memories of the past, or forgetting her recent experiences. Both were not at all pleasant to her in this life. "*Where would be Julian and Giselle?*" She laughed at the kind of question she asked. It was not that kind of thinking she usually had or believed. From the smile to the reflection, "*How would they be, Julian and Giselle?*" Then her countenance returned to the normal consistency of contempt and intolerance for life. She saw perfectly in her mind the image of Julian at the beginning of his decomposition, lying in his dark coffin. It was such a process of exhumation created by her imagination, that still carried the odors of dried flowers and of the gasses that accumulated around that deteriorating human figure. As for Giselle, shortly afterwards, in the same way she saw it clearly. White and dry, she lost her rosy, bright tone she had before in a death´s grimace. She stood up, satisfied with this.

That afternoon, she went to college to collect her belongings at the wardrobe locker. She returned about night, and after all, it was the right time to enter the Athos network. Her daily ritual from dusk until dawn.

That night, specifically, close to three o´clock AM, one person posted an unusual invitation. It was a proposal for a meeting the next night. A surprise meeting in a local so unusual to her that someone would suggest. Her costume was formally indicated, and if she wanted to invite someone else, she would be free and allowed. Patricia, in that moment of reading, laughed at her solitude. That´s couldn´t be called a party, properly speaking, but Patricia finally smiled at the initiative. She confirmed her presence and waited for the address at that event.

She sent a direct message to Charles, asking if he would attend this event. But she had no answer. Then she tried Sinead, and in the same way, it was in vain… But close to the sunrise, Sinead answered her.

- This event is more localized,
First of all, pay attention to the address.
It can be in another city or state.
But if this is in your area, do everything to come
by, and be present!
There is always so much fun! Kss"

Patricia went to bed, looking different that day. A little joy could be seen in her eyes and her place was almost in a perfect order. She was somehow happy, but tired. All that work withdrew her ability to stay awake and aware of what she was doing. So much so that when she went to bed, that subject about the physical encounter of the virtual friends of the network confused her mind. She didn´t know if it was going to happen, or whether it had happened the day before. She fell asleep.

24th Week

At night she was wearing the only dress left, which also was her only available clothes. Little crumpled and smelled of kept, but clean. According to her stagnant social life, it was a sad coincidence.

While she´d tried to put on makeup, she was listening to music from her laptop. Black Sabbath´s - Planet Caravan. She walked over and over around the room as she thought about the sequence of things she still had to do before leaving. She stopped in front of the mirror and watched for a moment. A short time, but enough to punish herself for a silly smile. *"Such an idiot!"* She would be like a teenager on her first date. She turned back her traditional tone of seriousness and continued to dress. Unhurried.

She turned off the light when she came out the door. Wearing her black dress she went to meet some real virtual friends. She was excited about the possibility of having a relevant social event. There was a lot to talk about and a lot to hear from those people who she found really interesting.

The taxi stopped right in front of the door of a charming but unknown pub. Nor even the driver knew the existence of that establishment there. She had to speak the name three times and indicate twice the correct address. Even with the mistakes of twists and turns, it was a quiet journey to Asp.

She left the taxi right at the front door with neon and an old fashioned decoration in a kilt style as well. At the entrance a doorman who appeared to be close to ninety years old smiled at her and then opened the entrance door. It was a dark corridor with led lights on the floor. There was not much light but a dim lighting coming from the end of the corridor where she could see a corner to the left. She walked toward that dim light. As the music increased, she couldn't saw where the wall, the floor, and the ceiling were either. Finally, arriving at the turn of the corridor she was surprised, misunderstanding how long the crossing of a single corridor lasted. At the junction leading to another door, there was a mirror partially covered by black veils and electric candles side by side. She stopped there to see herself for a few moments before entering.

Her shape in the mirror was perfect. Body, hair, make-up and clothes. Everything was perfect as she had imagined it from the start. Shiny silky hair, bright smile and makeup. She sighed with a flash of vanity. However, so fixed only in her forms and appearance, she didn't realize a small peculiarity of that mirror. It did not reflect the rest of the corridor and the door it's behind. Neither lights nor texture of the walls, only a black and endless void. Only the emphasized reflection of the presence of Patricia.

She tugged on her lipstick again and turned toward the main door to the pub's interior. Without realizing that in the mirror she would still be reflected in an image of her that looked at her with interest and disdain at the same time. The image faded to a grayish spot with spots characteristic of a human skull. She finally turned and went back into the darkness of the mirror from where it came.

She touched the door handle that led into the pub, but before she listened to the music playing. *"I knew this song!"* – Total Eclipse of the Heart by Bonnie Tyler, she smiled and opened the door thinking to see a place full of people and young people like her.

She saw a circular dance floor with two dancing couples and a few busy tables with silent people. And in the background a drowsy bartender who watched people with his tiny mustache and hair full of gel. Although somewhat disappointed, she was walking slowly trying to recognize some familiar face of them, but the lights flashed between blue and red casting shadows over people who seemed to be hiding.

Sitting alone at a table near the dance floor realized that couples were very unusual! The first one was a very fat man who danced with a very thin boy with effeminate air and the other couple was composed of an old lady who danced with a very tall gentleman who seemed to be over forty years old. *"Only forty years old..."* She smiled at the irony of the age difference between them. When the music ended, the couple of men were hugged to their table and the couple disbanded and went each to their respective table. They were not together at all.

A brief silence... Another song began to play. She didn't know that, but she knew it was an old song too. A little more rocking began to pay attention to the lyrics. *"I was made for love you baby..."* She liked the mood the music gave the place and felt excited to get her a drink. She went to the bar and ordered vodka on ice. The bartender stared at her before asking how old she was. She felt a little flattered by the waiter's doubt and confirmed her full nineteen, almost twenty years old. The bartender didn't want to check any papers and turned to prepare her drink at once.

With her drink, she turned to the table with hopes of making her night into something very pleasant. As she sat down, a middle-aged lady came to meet her to ask something:

- Hello! My name is Jessica and it's me and my husband at that table. She jerked with her chin as she continued. If you want to join us, it will be my pleasure.

Patricia smiled and thanked her, but said she was there because of a face-to-face meeting of her friends from a social network. The woman listened to her patiently and then said:

- Yes darling! All of us here are from your network. Join us! She caught Patricia softly by the arm with her lean, cold hand as she held her drink with the other hand. The two of them went through the place to the destination table.

As she sat down, she greeted the gentleman in front and noticed that he would be old enough to be Jessica's father. However, everything there seemed surreal to her. She introduced herself and began to answer some questions: age, where she was born, what she did... Things like that. As soon as she was socially acclimated, she had the courage to ask about the pub and the other presents.

- Ohh, don´t mind, so. They are unfortunate! Jessica said with a gesture.

- But they are such different people! - Patricia insisted.

- Calm down little girl, you still have not seen anything yet! You must wait until midnight, when all the other guests were expected. - Jessica said that as she tried to light a cigarette. Her husband only turned and smiled.

- But "unfortunate"…why? Didn't they have fun, did they? - She took another sip.

- Hell yes! A lot of fun! As if there was not much fun to have on. For some of them it is a first reunion after several years. Don´t you see the two at the table? - Jessica pointed the finger without much ceremony.

Patricia turned and recognized the pair of men who had just danced.

- So they are a couple? - She asked curiously.

- Not a couple at all, they're father and son. They were scheduled to meet here after long years of longing. That's why these face-to-face meetings are for, to end all our homesickness and feel free and alive from time to time! - She laughed within the smoke.

Patricia felt sorry for both of them as she watched their caresses gesture made each other. It was sounding *Loosing my Religion* by REM, when more guests were come in. Some of them came alone, just like her, and many others were in pairs. Anything seemed usual in that place!

In the midst of her impressions, a very thin lady arrived at the table and bowed to Patricia and said:

- I heard about your two friends. If you're willing to open up and tell me the details, I'll be happy to help you. - She spoke in a calm, leisurely voice.

Jessica and her husband had got up to dance, so Patricia smiled at her and motioned for the chair to sit down. The woman sat down and Patricia, no longer paying attention to the place surrounding her, began to tell her recent anxieties and fears. About her anger against the world and the need for more financial resources. At that moment, or maybe anticipating the kind of complaint of Patricia, the lady opened her purse and said:

- Here, take whatever you need. - Presenting her with a considerable pack of money.

Patricia watched the pack moving in front of her eyes. - Then she looked at the lady.

- I cannot accept it! - She said it looking down.

- They are yours somehow. - She set the pack on the table and said.

- I'll soon move to Giselle's apartment and hope you can help me with the displacement.

Patricia was very impressed by the total amount of money she saw, but she´s got a mixed feeling of having someone from her network living in a familiar place, and being able to help someone. Although, she felt fragile and weaker before that lady.

Her name was Polianne, and she was a recent widow due to her husband's death. She just could not tell when it was.

Close to midnight, the whole dance floor was already occupied. Jessica was dancing with her husband and there were other couples swinging by Elton John's Goodbye Yellow Brick Road. They seemed happy and sad at the same time. Patricia was also in that vibe. Glad to have met real people and at same time sad for being alone. No matter how many people there were, she felt helpless. She sought at least the semblance of her closest friends: Sinead and Charles. But what she saw the most was a parade of strangers in sober clothes and women in vintage clothes, each with a style that is gone.

When the couple returned to the table, Jessica wanted to continue the conversation about the other people she already seemed to recognize very well.

- The skinny young man who danced with his father... Would he like to dance with me?" - Patricia insinuated herself to Jessica.

Jessica made a loud laugh.

- No, dear, the oldest was the boy. He was the father of his fat boy who grew old after him. The son is really an old man and the father is a young man. Nothing here seems like you used to see!

Patricia thought Jessica would already be under the influence of alcohol for the answer, but then she could see that people's reactions were not related to her appearance or age. They were for the most part family members who reviewed each other after being separated for years and their age no longer mattered at that moment.

She sipped her third cup of vodka, hoping that nightmare shall pass quickly.

25th Week

Patricia was looking at those wooden boxes that had come from the moving of her new friend. She was going to officially occupy the apartment belonging to Giselle. Amidst a small commotion between two other locals who complained about the noise on the stairs.

They were disagreeing with their point of views, in some kind of hard discussion. Those were blaming each other on a never-ending wrangle. Such discordance should have already existed between them, but which had been incited by the noises of recent displacement. Nothing made sense in that duel which disrupted Patricia's concentration.

- Small old boxes, big, heavy boxes, dark wooden boxes... Nothing was absolutely familiar in that baggage without luggage instead. However, the instructions were accurate in her post:

> "Please check they may have
> disposed my belongings inside my new apartment,
> I arrive at 11:58 PM today - Poly."

Inside an envelope left under her door, a note that anticipated thanks, and more eight hundred Dollars in cash for expenses, according to that note. *"How about expenses?!"* She thought this might be returned to Polianne as soon as she arrived.

In the middle of the afternoon, she was sitting next to Milena, but they didn't talked each other for weeks. Something was definitely not going so well in that relationship. Milena was more comprehensive than Patricia, but she was frustrated with the unfolding of her friend's life and her own condition also.

Patricia, oblivious to all this, was scouring her e-mail box and finding out the same: spam, offers, old messages... But there was an old email from Giselle that apparently was sent and lost. "*to open or not to open...*" She was trying to convince herself that reading would be useful.

When she opened it, she saw a text written in up case letters trying to alert her to something. As much as she concentrated, she could not read the nexus of those words. But some words caught his attention:

"CAUTION! PATRÍCIA A GREAT DANGER! THEY KILL JULIAN HERE IN MY PLACE! I FEAR FOR YOUR MY FRIEND. GET AWAY, GET OFF THE CITY, GET OUT NOW! YOUR FRIENDS ARE DEAD! ONE BY ONE, ARE DEAD, EVERYONE. YOU ALSO, WE, ALL OF US! "

As much as she read, it didn't look like Giselle was writing, it's look like someone else. *"- How about so dead?"*; *"Who killed Julian, after all?"*

She was more confused by the reading, but much more by the hands that were around her head. Four silhouettes of pairs of hands floated lightly on her temples, across her neck and over her head, in an attempt to magnetize her thoughts. Those hands ministered to Patricia high doses of negative energy, capable of leaving her scattered and confused. Even more than she already was. Those hands could not be clearly seen, but for a closer look, Patricia's hair was seen to be electrified and getting upright as they took these attempts.

At the attentive glances of Milena, Patricia was becoming sadder and confused by these revelations. There was nothing she could do to save her friend from this state of despair and disenchantment.

One of these hands slid down Patricia's arm and landed on her cell-holding hand. Turned to the left, slightly lower and induced a tab. Soon the email was deleted and possibly Patricia would not remember her content within a few hours. For the first time that whole month she had much sleep at the afternoon.

It was close to four o'clock PM, and Patricia threw herself on the floor of Polianne's apartment, falling asleep. She was powerless and prostate, while her cellphone still turned on, almost out charge. The screen was closed for a standby module and a red LED was light on that device. For long minutes and as the fading light of sunset finally went through a window, that red led doubled. Two little red lights at the bottom of a room were the only lights can been seen. In an eye shape formed that tried to illuminate that growing darkness.

When she woke up it was later at night and she was not frightened by it. She was only puzzled by the cold of the room. Her thinness and her clothes were not enough to contain the chills and tremors. She guessed being hungry and at the same time remembered Polianne's arrival. So the sensation of being hungry had no priority she guessed. She was more focused on the event than proper food. She smiled at herself for that lack of health and finally went in search of food, after all she should be able to help the new friend to settle.

At exactly ten past eleven o'clock PM the alarm of her cellphone rang and Patricia left her piece of pizza aside in half. It was time to prepare for the meeting with Polianne at her new address.

A sequence of knocks on the door could be heard at precisely two minutes to midnight. Closer to the door, she looked through the spy eye and found Polianne standing with her backs toward the door, looking down to the corridor in front of her. Before Patricia touched the doorknob, she turned to her and smiled as if she had not before. She entered.

Patricia was speaking during Polianne's inspection of the rooms, wanting to know more about the positive and negative questions of living there on that city region and her neighbors. As they passed the door of her future room, which had the door quite opened, Polianne stopped and stared through the gap of the door to the interior of the room. Something between curiosity and familiarity.

- What's it? Patricia asked suspiciously.

- Nothing. I was just looking. - Polianne answered after a brief moment. She spoke without turning to Patricia.

They continued checking the place out until the door of the guesting room and Polianne stopped and asked:

- Did you do what I asked you to do with the boxes? - Her tone had changed.

- Yeah, it's all in there. - Patricia trying to be friendly. - I didn't mess anything, as you wish.

- Great! You will sleep here with me today. And later come here in my room, there will be a visit I want to introduce you, ok? - She tried to be nice.

- Of course it will be a pleasure. I knock at your door. OK? - Still thinking about the discomfort of the night she's going to pass in there.

- Anyway! Just open it. The door will be unlocked. She said that just as she had finally opened her door and closed it, leaving Patricia outside in the corridor

Those brief moments between the opening of the door and its closure, it was enough for Patricia to find out the source of her cold sensation. It came from Polianne's dark room, which surprised Patricia as a breath of iced air. But much more than the sense of intense cold she felt was the frightening deepest darkness in the room. It was in that Polianne threw herself as she closed the door behind her.

Patricia hugged herself, wrapping her arms as went to the direction of her room, with no looking back. With no thoughts about the origins of such darkness, or who really would be the person of Polianne, her new "friend" gave her direction and energy for her recent decisions. She did want to return home, and wanted to return to her familiar and comfortable room. Such a heaven, after all.

She was lying over old newspapers, when her cell phone vibrated with the one o'clock AM alarm, she quickly became aware of what had to come. Something, or rather someone, was acting as a counselor so she would not be late to meet Polianne and her guest friends.

In wanting to not look so sloppy for the eyes of strangers, she searched for a mirror in the bathroom. But as she settled in, she remembered Milena and her father clearly. Strangely, it was as if they were seeing her right inside the bathroom. She looked around to check out and it was empty. It was the same, white and calm.

In front of the mirror, she hoped that a little makeup could give her a sense of youth she had before when she arrived in the city. But there was not even a lipstick to use, nor even a step back in time. At that moment, with no certainty, she was observing a woman who would be leaving this life forever and seeing her body returned to the world of matter, feeding her atoms and molecules back to the ground. She hoped that the transformation of decomposition could erase once and for all her useless and fruitless existence.

For a few moments, she shuddered as she glimpsed to look with her fingers that couldn't take care of her lips, eyelashes, and eyelids anymore. Those were just bones! But not for cold or for weakness, just because, for a moment, her imagination just mixed the image reflection in the mirror and showed her what was really beneath the skin. Her lips were summed up in fine traces of compound flesh, partially overcoming her exposed teeth without gums in a perfect death skull. Her eyes lost their color and brilliance, leaving for dry pits with no flesh around them, revealing that almost nothing will remain for a day.

In a sort of trance, nourished by her nocturnal counselors, Patricia let herself be taken in a sad tune of surrender to her destination. Her time had come, she should move on to the other world, where she could really be happy at once. In a brief instant, just one spark!

From the top of the sink, his cellphone fell to the floor after receiving a message that made it vibrate. It had spread some parts on the bathroom floor and Patricia, still scared, tried to collect it. After restarting the device, she tried to see whose message it was.

"How strange, Giselle!" She didn't agree with the sender of the message and thought it would be a bad joke or someone was trying to frighten her.

"Good night my friend, I know we can meet soon.
There was an authorization here,
so I'll come and see you!
Kisses, I miss you very much!"

Someone should have taken Giselle's cellphone or her chip, and she'd be playing a joke on it. She was angrier than I'm afraid of. She tried to erase that message.

At last, the moment had come. She checked her appearance again and headed to the door. But strangely every step she took, it seemed that her door was further away. She did not understand this sudden change of her senses. It was an extended projection of the room, as if it was the corridor leading to Polianne's room. The floor at her feet was absorbing her footsteps and turning each one into a new path to the door. *"Or would it be Polianne's door?"* She paused to be sure what was happening. Her head was spinning and the corridor even more spinning around her. She cried out to herself, but her throat was making no sound: *"Enough!"* So she found herself facing the door of Polianne's room.

"Yes, it was that!" She would be sure from some internal noise that room with an ear close to the door, before she timidly knocked the door. Nothing.

The door creaked slightly, when Patricia saw Polianne smiling at her in the doorway. She kissed her and they went inside. She entered a deeply familiar place like that would be her own room, but it was completely inverted. Just like in a mirror, what should have been on the left was on the right. The bed is placed on the opposite wall. The desk was on the "wrong" side; the bathroom at the other end of the room... The color and tonality she would swore she was in her room in the boarding house, but in a version completely opposite to its conception. It took some minutes more to feel comfortable. While this, Polianne prepared her some drink.

- They're almost arriving! - She said cheerfully.

- Who are they? - She asked as she took the glass with one hand, with no looking at Polianne.

- They are two friends of ours who were at the party. They are from our virtual network and you will love to meet them! She sat down upon the bed and bedside her.

While sipping that strange drink, Patricia paid attention to the song that played in the background: The Doors' Riders on the Storm. The light was fainter, and the weight of the some kind of alcohol in the drink was immediately apparent to her as she felt her lips numb and an easy sensation of relaxation.

Polianne was talking about her deceased husband and her impressions of death when they suddenly knocked at the door. Polianne, didn't say anything. Just got up, left her room and went to open the door for the newcomers. Quite numb, Patricia didn't miss the lack of manners of her hostess and took the opportunity to lay down on the bed with her arms over her head. Everything was deliciously different, colors, smells, memories and sounds. Nothing else seemed like it was before. She remembered her childhood, her grandmother, her father, the first kiss... Until she heard a sweet voice calling to her:

- Patricia, are you ok, darling? - Polianne bent over her with her guests standing beside the bed.

Patricia, still under the influence of her memories, asked her grandmother for a blanket to go to bed. It was late! That sweet voice...

No my girl, I'm Polianne! Get up a little to see our friends.

- Now? - Complained about that lazy girl from years ago.

- Yes, honey, now! - She caught and pulled Patricia by both arms to lift her.

Patricia smiled at her new friends and didn't find her clothes too strange, or were they using fantasies? They looked like they were going to a mask party. She began to laugh compulsively.

She was delirious when she was raised to dance with her new friends, while Polianne told them things in a strange language that both could easily understand. They held her in their arms, making seductive movements from one side to the other. In a dance of three, Patricia held her friend's neck in front of her as the reptile one standing behind her grasped her waist, synchronizing a movement with her hips. Patricia's hand reached for her new dog-it friend's neck and pulled her head close to her ear. She wanted action, wanted to caress, caresses of someone like them, tall and strong, no matter how hideous and menacing.

She was already half-naked, when Polianne brought a small bag of surgical medical equipment from Patricia's belongings. She opened it and placed a scalpel at her hand.

At that moment, she danced alone to Whitesnake's - Is This Love? song, staring at the scalpel, fixed on its brightness. Eyes of a silver snake, she raised it in the air with both hands above her head. She danced and looked at its rattlesnake with lust and seduction. She wrapped herself in its sinuosity, throwing her legs and hips to the both sides slowly on the rhythm. While Polianne watched her, sat and surrounded by two friends lying on the floor, watching this burlesque show in honor of death.

Patricia licked the tip of her scalpel, with an interest in exchanging saliva with the snake's tongue she thought she was holding. A kiss of death on a mortal object. It passed slowly on the tip of her tongue and a small wound filled with blood. It ran down her chin as her tongue came in and out of her mouth, licking the strange living object. The two tongues now bifurcated, touched and intertwined, in a mixture of pleasure and pain.

The dog-it and the alligator now looked at Polianne who caressed them with her hands. They were in a privileged position to see the show of that macabre dance.

Patricia now passed the serpent's head in sinuous signs on her chest and belly. Scratching now, sometimes cutting into traces that meant words of a forgotten and ancient language. The snake returned the absorbed heat, with more traces of blood added and made the bar of Patricia's panties spattered with blood.

Patricia dropped to her knees with her body turned back, offering her viewers the sight of her bloody pubis underneath her panties. She blushed frantically, when the snake decided to enter her body, looking for the navel, where it made a small force to occupy its new burrow. Patricia bowed arched with the pain of the snake's bite that quickly sought the comfort of her warm body. Once in contact with her bowels, it was held there by the warmth of Patricia's blood.

Exactly at the end of the song, Polianne and her friends were applauding Patricia's performance, which rose up panting, sweaty, and satisfied with her deed.

She went to his friends and welcomed them with affectionate hugs and kisses. She was happy, slightly happy as she never felt before. It seems that the effect of the drink and its artistic presentation have taken away from it a weight of shyness and worry. She went to the bathroom to wash and came back wet and clean. Ready to wear dry clothes again.

She went to the other room, it was already two o'clock AM when she lay in her bed. She slept a quiet and serene sleep. And she dreamed.

She dreamed of a nursing faculty, a chance to study, and a network of virtual friends. She dreamed of real friends and dreamed of the end of pain.

Epilogue

The old boarding house had been closed for months. After the facts reported in the newspapers, nobody else had the interest of staying in that property that's why it was for sale.

But much more disturbing was the general state of the building where Giselle lived. There were three horrible deaths in less than forty days. A fact that left the authorities intrigued and the building abandoned.

Inside that still could be felt a slight atmosphere of the recent death of something once been alive. Dust, peeling walls, nails on the doors, sheets of paper with little notes, trash and shadows. People fled hurriedly, leaving behind a trail of objects, papers, and fragments of life, while still possessing it.

From the last place of Patricia remained an empty and dirty room. Something that one day was filled with her presence, but today is a dark place in an old and condemned building. There she slept, wept, and prepared for life that no longer belonged to her.

How long had she been dead? By the state in which her body was found, there were at least three weeks. No more than that. The son of the building owner was the first person I could open the apartment and get into the darkened room.

However in her room at the boarding house, annotations and her electronic devices were taken away by the police for investigation. They wanted to understand all that context of pain and violence that involved the young woman's death and whether she would have a connection with the others. *"Was she a serial killer?"*

In her notes, details about routine, her studies and about the people she hated. In her personal archives, endless stories chronicled her sad end and how she identified herself with dead people.

Each piece studied in Anatomy gave a strange name. Every day of the week she described encounters with her imaginary "friends." In each email she sent there are requests and recommendations to some kind of beings to kill her classmates. One after one, by the exact college presence list, she had a copy, which was killed in her notes and emails.

However, the police had not yet found relations or further indications of two people who were always presented by Patricia as their "angels". On the other hand, when they looked for files about whoever she called her "friends," nothing made sense.

Pages after pages of ex-dead employees who once worked in college have been attached to this case. Profiles, pictures, data... All of them still seemed to have close and daily contact with Patricia. She had written passages and e-mails exchanged with people who died in the 1940s, or 1960s for example.

The pages were stained in blood in her notebook, several mentions to three "enemies" she had. Drawings of beings with horns and claws. Snakes with faces of dogs and alligators. Knives and scalpels that cut veins and tissues. She looked like a very tormented person who could imagine conversations and dialogues with the dead people at all.

The most frequent and scrawled names were "Sinead" and "Charles", considered by her as executioners. Beings she believed were sent to kill her and bring her enslaved soul into a dimension of pain and suffering.

On some other pages, there were drawings and phrases about "Milena" (unidentified) and "Rudolph" (unidentified) who had wings and flowers in their hands. She left lipstick marks, that were proven to be recognized as hers, in letters and tickets never been sent to this one called "Rudolph". Possibly a case of affective relationship projection.

But nothing would be compared to what she described as "*Supreme Being*." An unknown woman called her "Polianne". It seemed for most of the agents, the representation of evil for the fragile Patricia's mind. This kind of ghost would be above other two evil spirits indicated in the previous pages by her. Polianne had about fifteen pages dedicated exclusively to the fanciful narratives, in which she introduced and lived with Polianne.

Her identified dead cause was hypovolemic shock, affected by many incisions and cuts from his tongue, to his belly at the groin. They were shallow, punctual and long cuts. They wrote unknown letters and symbols in every body part. The photographs of the cuts and scalpel used were describing a slow self-mutilation that should have consumed at least twelve last hours of the victim's life.

In her papers, several receipts from her father and mother who sent her money weekly during those six months she tried to take her nursing course at that large city. They just could not understand why she would not have attended classes with assistance or at least get her final exams done.

On her laptop, hundreds of posts saved in folders with strange names were found: Pain, Fear, Sex, Sadism, Terror, Shadows, Hate... For every human sensation of extreme tension, there seemed to be a folder with many photos, files, texts , gifs and videos. They scanned the search sites and none of those files recognized the source sites or even the public domain.

In those folders were two with further information with several clues to understand the death of Julian and its connection with the death of Giselle.

But the greatest doubt was: How did a schizophrenic girl achieve a content so qualified to generate her suicide, very intellectually grounded? She would need a network of knowledge, or connected minds aligned to evil just to let it happen.

But much more than perplexed, all agents were intimately shaken and frightened in their convictions and faith. When they picked up all the audios recorded on Patricia's cellphone, a message she had recorded and sent, exactly one day after her death:

"Better than loving the dead, it is being loved by them!"

And the rest was an inaudible wheezing until the silence presented itself in its tone of dark emptiness.

ABOUT THE AUTHOR

Mr. Machado, Eduardo B. (MsC) was born in mystical Brazil, and carries his fears since 1970. Business consultant, university professor and researcher, after many technical books for the business world, the dark side may have to call him to write about horror and gothic novels.

After twenty-four years of Catholicism, he began his experience with spiritual cults and Kardecism. Most of his content is some real story from the other side of life, where he usually gets inspiration.

He lives alone and uses the suffering and pain of others to continue his curse and explore the unspoken sensations and dark emotions that surround us every day, or rather, every night.

With eight published works, including the Loneliness Network trilogy, also published in Portuguese, he has already made his debut with a suspense piece of work and now brings all the refinement of a mind that seeks its rebalancing through the fantastic, the imaginary and the pain in a work that explores different facets of death in these four tales.

OTHER WORKS

- ✠ The Loneliness Network – Book I: Agnostic (www.amazon.com)
- ✠ The Loneliness Network – Book II: Apprentix (www.amazon.com)
- ✠ The Loneliness Network – Book III: Agonic (www.amazon.com)
- ✠ The Manufacture of Death (www.amazon.com)
- ✠ True Projections, Fake Intentions (www.amazon.com)